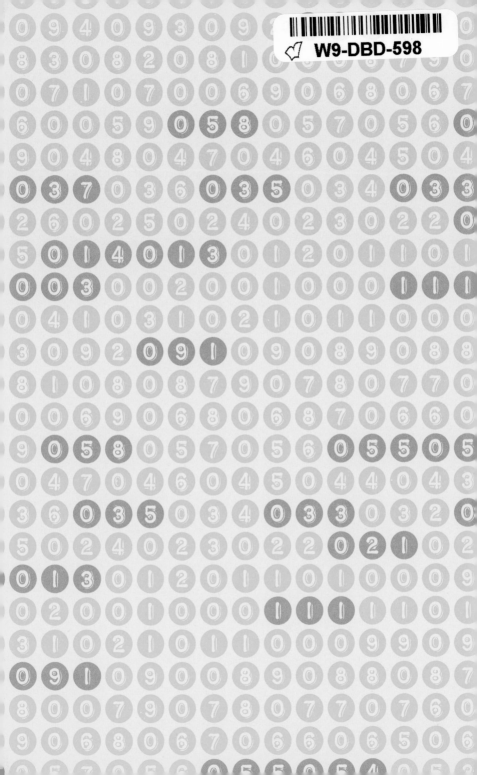

HOW I STOLE
JOHNNY DEPP'S
ALIEN GIRLFRIEND

HOW I STOLE *JOHNNY*

DEPP'S ALIEN GIRLFRIEND

BY GARY GHISLAIN

chronicle books · san francisco

Library of Congress Cataloging-in-Publication Data
Ghislain, Gary.
  How I stole Johnny Depp's alien girlfriend / by Gary Ghislain.
     p. cm.
  Summary: Fourteen-year-old David, the son of a famous French psychologist, falls in love
with Zelda, a new patient who believes she is from outer space, and soon they are tearing
through Paris in search of her chosen one, Johnny Depp, so that she can take him to her
home planet, Vahalal.
  ISBN 978-0-8118-7460-1 (alk. paper)
  [1. Extraterrestrial beings—Fiction. 2. Mental illness—Fiction. 3. Juvenile delinquency—
Fiction. 4. Depp, Johnny—Fiction. 5. Paris (France)—Fiction. 6. France—Fiction.] I. Title.
  PZ7.G3390236How 2011
  [Fic]—dc22
  2010034927

Book design by Jennifer Tolo Pierce.
Typeset in Apollo MT, Big Noodle Titling, Dingos, and Monster Mash.
The illustrations in this book were rendered using digital medium.

Manufactured by C & C Offset, Longgang, Shenzhen, China, in April 2011.

10 9 8 7 6 5 4 3 2 1

This product conforms to CPSIA 2008.

Chronicle Books LLC
680 Second Street, San Francisco, California 94107

www.chroniclekids.com

FOR ILO AND SISKO, MY TWO
FAVORITE SPACEGIRLS IN THE ENTIRE UNIVERSE . . .
AND BEYOND!

EXPIRATION: 111 HOURS

There are a few things everybody knows about Zelda:

1. They caught her stealing food in a supermarket just outside Paris.

2. She was "scantily dressed" in some sort of . . . let me see . . . "futuristic fetish outfit."

3. She resisted arrest and sent two security guys to the hospital with concussions and a few broken bones.

4. They couldn't find her relatives, or any sign of a past, or anyone who knew her—like she had just fallen from the sky.

Which makes it *that* much more interesting when she says she's from outer space.

———————

I've been passing by Dad's office again and again, pretending to go to the bathroom but really trying to get a good look at her through the open door.

Here's the extra data I've gathered during my expeditions:

5. She has long, dark-blond hair. It's curly and messy, and she keeps hiding her eyes behind it.

6. Regarding the eyes: I managed to see them when she blew her hair sideways to take a good look back at me. They're green and mean.

7. She's pretty in a scary sort of way. Like something you'd really like to touch but that will probably bite.

8. Oh, and she's very tall for a girl. I think she's quite thin, too but it's hard to tell because she's wearing the oversize, worn-out jeans and sweater they give them at the juvenile detention center. I'd say she's about fifteen or sixteen, but she told Dad she's three hundred twenty-five—that's three hundred twenty-five years on her planet.

I decide to make another round trip to the toilet. She has moved her hair sideways, like she knew I was coming.

"Why are you staring at me like that?"

"I'm not staring at you." I point toward the bathroom. "I live here. I was just passing by."

"So keep on passing by, DWARF!"

The policewoman sitting next to her jerks her handcuffs.

I walk away and lock myself in the bathroom.

Dwarf? Pfft!

I'm only fourteen. I might still be growing.

Dad lives on a farm in the middle of nowhere—nowhere being the very edge of Normandy, one hundred miles from Paris. His village is surrounded by cornfields, apple trees, cows, and hateful villagers. The village is called Cornouaille. The villagers are called Cornouaillois, which is a ridiculous name and probably adds to their resentment.

The Cornouaillois hate Dad unanimously. He's from Paris, and he's a famous therapist, and that's more than enough to tick them off. They call him the "nutty professor" and his house the "nut farm" because of all the "troubled" teenagers the judge sends here to be fixed.

Now Dad's fixing Zelda.

———

"Is she crazy?" I ask.

Dad smiles. He's making her a hot chocolate and gazing at the cornfield beyond our back garden while the milk warms up. "No one is ever crazy, David."

I look down at the tray he's bringing her. He's not using the cheap chocolate cookies he usually gives patients. He's giving her *my* cookies! The fancy new crème brûlée ones I brought with me from Mom's place in Paris.

"Is she dangerous?"

"No, she's not dangerous."

"So why is she handcuffed in your office?"

"Mm? Good question, son." He blows gently on her hot chocolate, thinking it over. "You're right, it does show very little trust. I'll take the handcuffs off tonight."

———

I'm having a nightmare where Zelda asks me to cut off her hands to remove her handcuffs when I'm awakened by a commotion downstairs.

As I leave my room, I see two uniformed policemen arguing with Dad down in the foyer. A train conductor has been beaten up. Zelda has escaped. They brought her back.

"She's a demon, a tigress, THE DEVIL!" one of the policemen tells Dad.

I sit down at the top of the stairs, where no one can see me.

"She escaped because she thinks she's here on a mission," Dad explains.

But the policemen don't care what sort of nuts she is. They don't want Zelda to beat up any more train conductors.

"Use the damn shackles and lock her in her room!"

"I will," Dad concedes. "But she'll escape again. Her drive is *that* strong."

You can hear the pride in Dad's voice. It must be very annoying for the policemen.

Dad offers them coffee—or something stronger, like a Cognac or a local Calvados.

One of the policemen relaxes the second a Cognac lands in his hand. "She's not your everyday little girl." He empties his glass in a single gulp. "Took four of our guys to immobilize her. Two of them are lying in the hospital as we speak."

"She's tough," Dad agrees, and refills their glasses.

———

I'm alone, eating my second serving of Coco Pops. Dad's still sleeping, recovering from last night's madness. I made him a pot of coffee and toasted some bread, hoping the smell would wake him up so I can keep grilling him about Zelda. In the meantime, I flip through the letters the postman just dropped on the kitchen table. I'm trying to find the exciting ones, like Dad's daily hate mail. Last summer, Dad received two rabbit heads in a shoebox. The villagers would love to see him and the nut farm gone, and they don't mind wasting a rabbit or two to let him know.

One letter catches my eye because of the funny snake logo and the thick, fancy paper. It's been addressed to Dad's office in Paris and forwarded here. I open it. It's another cuckoo message about Zelda. We've gotten plenty of those since Dad was on TV to talk about his work with her. It's just a few words beautifully handwritten on the thick sheet of paper: *Let the Traveler go. Zelda belongs with us. First warning.* It's signed "The Sanctuary" with an *S* like a snake.

I quickly put the letter back in its strange envelope and drop it on the table when I hear Dad coming out of his room, yawning loudly.

He grabs a cup of coffee, sits at the table, and reaches to gently stroke my hair.

"Why did you tell them she's on a mission?" I ask, pouring extra milk over my Coco Pops.

Dad looks up from his coffee cup. The pouches under his eyes are two shades darker than usual. "Were you listening last night?"

I nod. It's no big surprise. Dad already knows how nosy I am.

"She's on some sort of quest," he explains.

"Like what?"

Dad never avoids a challenging question. He believes children deserve the truth, no matter what. I still regret asking him where babies come from at an age when most kids are perfectly happy with the stork theory.

"She's looking for a boyfriend."

Even my Coco Pops stop popping.

"Or a soul mate, if you like," Dad says, buttering a cold piece of toast. "She calls him her 'chosen one,' and she believes he's waiting for her, somewhere . . . *around here.*"

He draws a large circle with the butter knife. By "around here," he means Earth.

2
EXPIRATION: 91 HOURS

"I told you to leave me alone, dwarf."

Zelda's sitting on the floor in Dad's office, pulling hard on her shackles like she's trying to break the chain tying her ankle to the couch.

"I'm not a dwarf. I'm only fourteen. I'm still growing."

She stops yanking on the shackles and turns around to give me a mean green look. "Same thing. You're *small*."

She gives the shackles a serious pull. *Clank!*

"There's no point doing that. They're not going to break."

She gives a series of even stronger pulls. *Clank! Clank! Clank!* Even the couch must have felt those.

"Stop it. You're just hurting yourself."

She closes her eyes and lies down, breathing heavily. "Are you going to stare at me like that all day?"

"I'm not staring. I was on my way to see Olivier before you started dismembering yourself."

She reopens her eyes. "What is *Olivier*?"

"My friend. Our neighbor. He's fourteen, too."

"Another dwarf!"

"He's actually quite tall."

She sits up, rubbing her ankle.

"He's a bit fat, too."

Out of nowhere, she flips around and lands on all fours, looking straight into my eyes.

"His mother says he's big boned." I take a step back. She looks kind of threatening. "And he had a real girlfriend last year at summer camp. You can ask him: Kissing a girl is like kissing raw chicken."

I'm not usually this talkative.

"Raw chicken?"

"Yeah, all weird and gooey."

She seems to think about this, then—*CLANK!*—she leaps forward. The couch, an iron monster of about a gazillion tons, jumps forward a good half inch, and I'm so startled I fall back on my butt in the corridor.

Here's another thing about Zelda: She's really stubborn.

———

"She wants a boyfriend."

"You mean she wants to have *sex*?" Olivier says *sex* with the excitement you normally associate with climbing Mount Everest.

"Dad didn't say anything about that."

We're sitting in his garden, eating blue-cheese snacks and daydreaming about Zelda.

"Is she hot? Can we go see her?"

"No, we can't go see her. She's busy."

"Busy doing what?"

He snatches the pack of snacks while I try to come up with a good excuse to keep stalking Zelda on my own.

"She's busy getting fixed by Dad. They still have a lot of work to do."

He calls his dog, Pipette, the only creature besides me who can stand Olivier, and starts scratching him. I join in, even though I don't like Pipette very much. It's nothing personal. When I was four, Mom had a Doberman. It attacked me and chewed off half my face. I stayed a full year in a clinic where they fixed my looks. I have a long scar hidden under my hair and a small one on the left side of my nose to prove it.

I don't like dogs in general.

"Did you tell her I had a girlfriend at summer camp?"

"I sure did."

"Does she want to meet me, then?"

"Uh-uh. Negative."

He smiles widely, something you should never do while eating blue-cheese snacks. "I get it. You're scared."

"Scared of what?"

"Scared she can't resist my sex appeal and my moves." He demonstrates his "moves" by embracing an imaginary girl and giving her a series of soggy little kisses. "Are *you* going to kiss her, then?" he asks, dropping the poor imaginary girl on the ground.

"Who? Zelda? No! She's, like, dangerous." Pipette can't believe his luck: I've suddenly doubled my scratching speed.

"I mean, she's in your home. Locked. Handcuffed. Looking for a boyfriend." He leans so close I'm afraid he's going to try his moves on *me*. "Do it!"

"Do what?"

"Jump on her. Try to make out with her. She's, like, open territory, buddy."

Pipette runs away yapping. I've crossed the thin line between pleasure and pain.

"You think she would like that? Being jumped on?"

"Totally! Girls love that kind of stuff. Let's go shoot some frogs."

Dad doesn't want me to shoot frogs. He would rather talk about *why* I want to shoot them, which is way less fun. We go into Olivier's room for his air gun. I grab a new can of ammo from under his bed.

"She really believes she's from outer space?" he asks, getting his air gun from its hiding place under his mattress.

"Yes." I pass him the pellets and crawl deeper under the bed, reaching for his stash of comics.

Olivier is a DC fiend. I'm a Marvel guy. That's one of the many fundamental differences between us.

I look at the cover. Power Girl, flying high in the sky, a jetliner passing right under her. She stares at me with narrowed eyes, her face and body wrapped in her windblown platinum-blond hair and floating red cape.

Olivier crawls up beside me and picks up another Power Girl comic. "Is she anything like her?" He nods toward the cover. "You know, with the great bazooms."

"No, she's . . . she's just not like that."

"Can you imagine?" He kisses Power Girl on the cover. "A Supergirl living right next door in your house." He turns the pages to show me how *super* that would be. *Splash! Poom! Plop! Whiiiiz!* "Too bad your Spacegirl has small bazongas."

"She does not! They're . . ." I try to show him more or less with my hands. "Besides, she's not a Supergirl or a Spacegirl." I crawl out from under the bed. He's so annoying. I don't want him to talk about Zelda anymore, especially about bazooms and bazongas.

"So she's just nuts?" He gets out from under the bed, tossing the Power Girl comics on his duvet, probably for more kissing and contemplation later.

I nod, loading a pellet into the gun. "Yes. She's just nuts."

———————

There is a frog convention at the pond, but I don't have the heart to kill even one of them. I can't stop thinking about Zelda. Olivier gets annoyed and says I'm ruining the fun of killing frogs.

When I get back home, she's not in Dad's office anymore. She's sitting at the kitchen table, handcuffed to her chair while Dad's cooking lunch. She's playing with bread, making perfect little balls and lining them up on her plate.

"Are all the boys ugly on your planet?" I ask when Dad leaves us to get some wine from the cellar.

She adds another bread ball to the line. "There are no boys on Vahalal."

"What's Valala?"

"*Va-ha-lal* is the planet I come from, and men are forbidden on it."

"There's only girls on your planet?"

"Yes. It is what you Earthlings call paradise." She starts eating the bread balls.

"What would happen if I accidentally landed on your planet?" I look over my shoulder, making sure Dad is still going through his extensive collection of Burgundy. "Would I be some sort of king, being the only man?"

"As a *boy*, you would be destroyed immediately."

"Like . . . what? Killed?"

"More like vaporized by the Valks the instant you set foot on Vahalal." She illustrates by squeezing a bread ball into nothingness.

"What's a Valk?"

"Valks are fearless warriors and holy servants of Zook."

I want to laugh, because the Zooky-thingy sounds pretty funny. I don't. Dad's back, and the main rule in his house is *act normal when guests talk nuts.*

"Do you have wine on your planet?" I ask when Dad uncorks his bottle of Burgundy and helps himself to a very large glass.

"Alcohol as a form of entertainment has been banned since the fall of the fifth Primitive Empire." She collects a drop of wine sliding down the bottle with her finger and brings it to the tip of her tongue. "Phenolic acid, potassium, calcium, magnesium, sodium, iron, and . . . by Zook! You're drinking sulfites, Earthling!"

"Well"—Dad tastes the wine—"there are also lovely aromas of cherry, raspberry, and pear, don't you think?" He gulps down half the glass, totally ignoring her warning about the sulfites.

———

Dad's too tired for their afternoon session. He's gone to "read" in his office—meaning he's sleeping on his couch—and she's locked upstairs in her room like a prisoner.

My heart's racing as I try to get a peek at her through the keyhole. I can see a corner of her bed and one of her bare feet dangling over the edge.

"Why do you like watching me so much, dwarf?"

She must have some sort of radar.

"I'm not watching you. I just . . . I wanted to ask you something."

"What?"

She gets off the bed. Her eye appears right in front of mine on the other side of the keyhole. They're not just mean. They're beautiful, too.

"Why are men forbidden on your planet?"

"Men are a lower form of hominid," she answers, like it's obvious.

"What does that mean?"

"They're inferior to women, weak, dirty, and generally useless to the survival of our species."

"What about nice men? Or . . . nice boys?" (I.e., me.)

"Don't be absurd. There's no such thing."

"Why are you looking for a boyfriend, then?"

"It's my duty. I am a Traveler."

"What's a Traveler?"

No answer. Just her green eye staring at me. "Can you unlock the door?" she asks.

"I don't have the key."

"Can you get the key?"

It's on Dad's desk. And Dad's sleeping like a corpse. If I weren't such a good boy, I could easily get it and set her free.

"No, I can't get the key," I lie.

A brief silence and then, "You are useless, Earthling. Leave me alone." And the eye is gone.

Damn! We were just starting to develop a serious keyhole relationship.

"Don't you want someone to talk to?"

"Don't you have *toys* you need to play with?"

Okay, maybe I do. But they can wait. Because right now, I can't think of anything better than talking to her. I've glued my eye to the keyhole again: She's sitting on the bed, tearing a pillowcase.

"What are you doing with that pillow?"

A rope? A weapon? Fuel for a spaceship? No! A curtain! Against me!

She hangs it over my peephole. Show's over. Just when I wanted more.

I feel bad for Dad. The policemen were right. She's a demon, a tigress, THE DEVIL!

He took her out of her room for a late session, sat her in his office, and—*BANG!*—she jumped on him and smashed his iron elephant right on top of his head. I heard him cry for help, and when I came into the office, she was already running away across the garden, jumping over the fence like some kind of gazelle.

I'll tell you one thing: This girl's got legs.

I'm lying on my bed, contemplating the little fluorescent constellations, galaxies, and stars glued to the ceiling above me. She's so violent. I've never met a girl as violent as she is. Dad's the nicest person in the world. You cannot smash an iron elephant on the nicest man in the world's head!

I'm so angry at her. Spacegirl, my foot! She's just another thug with too much imagination, like all the nutcases Dad tries to fix!

Dad is downstairs waiting for the policemen to bring Zelda back. They caught her at a gas station outside Paris. She beat up a truck driver this time. Dad's so ashamed. Two violent escapes in two days: She's ruining his reputation as a friendly nutkeeper.

Knock knock.

I sit up on my bed. Dad comes in, carrying a large glass of Cognac. "Son?" he says, sitting beside me and sipping his drink. "I've changed my mind about Zelda. She might be dangerous." He has a bump the size of a chicken egg on top of his bald head to corroborate that fact.

"I can't have you here anymore," he says gently. "I'm phoning your mother. You're going back to Paris."

I don't know what's worse: leaving Zelda or going back to Mom and her tantrums for the rest of the summer.

"In the meantime, you must promise to stay away from Zelda, and that means not talking to her. At all."

There goes my favorite pastime.

"Promise me."

I do.

"Now I have to talk with your mom." Poor Dad. Talking with Mom is *not* his favorite pastime. He makes a face like one of his ulcers just popped.

"Why are you angry with me, dwarf?" she asks. "I didn't do anything to you."

"I'm not supposed to talk to you. I don't even *want* to talk to you," I lie.

Zelda sits down on the terrace floor, pulling on the gizmo locked on her ankle, trying to figure out how to get rid of it pronto. I'm staying at a safe distance, carefully monitoring her movements while pretending to be very busy fixing the back wheel of my bike.

She stops pulling at the gizmo. "I could have killed your father if I'd wanted to. I didn't. I rather like him." She picks up the apple Dad gave her earlier and sniffs it suspiciously. *Sniff sniff.* She decides it's food and bites off a large chunk. *Crunch crunch.*

"Interesting," she says, and goes back to working on the gizmo. "I asked him to remove my handcuffs and let me go. He would not. Knocking that artifact on his head was necessary protocol."

"Protocol?" I push the damn bike away, stand up, and give it a serious kick for good measure. "He's trying to help you. Do you understand that?"

"If he really wanted to help, he would let me go."

She can't escape anymore. She can't go farther than the terrace since the policemen locked the gizmo on her ankle. If she tries to leave again, it will go wild and they'll pick her up within minutes. Dad explained it to her: One more escape, and the judge will take her away from him and place her in a more conventional institution— like a proper nuthouse, with padded cells, straitjackets, and horse tranquilizers for afternoon snacks.

"Your father doesn't understand. I can't be here. I have a mission to complete and very little time left on this planet. What I did to him was unavoidable."

"It wasn't *unavoidable*!" I yell, turning away from her and going back to looking for the puncture on the tire. "You're not from another planet, Zelda. You're just another violent nutcase, and Dad's too nice to tell you so to your face."

Oh, I think I found the punc—OUCH!

She threw the apple at me, and it slammed into the back of my head.

"Pfft." She shakes her head. "It has interesting qualities as food, but it is too soft as a weapon."

Forget the bike. I stand up, rubbing the back of my neck. There must be steam coming out of my ears. "What did you do that for?"

"It felt right at the time."

I grab the apple and throw it back at her, but I don't have her talent. *Bang!* It ends up hitting Dad's office window.

"David?" Dad yells.

Shit. The apple interrupted Dad's "reading."

"I'm fixing my bike in the backyard!"

He comes out on the porch to check on us. "You remember what we agreed?"

He means avoiding Zelda like she's contagious until Mom finds the time to come pick me up.

"I'm waiting for you in my office," he tells Zelda. He has removed the elephant from his desk. He has also locked up his letter opener and his heavy stapler.

She picks up what's left of the apple on her way inside. "That was a really terrible throw, dwarf."

"I didn't take the time to aim."

Actually, I've never been good at throwing things. I'm not good at spitting, either. And Olivier always laughs at me because I can't burp on demand, but that's another story.

"See the hominid artifact all the way back there?" She points at the angel statue at the other side of the garden.

"No way! That's way too far!"

She sneers, bites off a large chunk of apple to bring her ammunition to the right weight, and throws it without even aiming. It flies like a bullet and explodes on the angel's face.

That's the most amazing thing I've seen since Olivier fell in the cemetery pond and nearly drowned.

"How did you do *that*?!"

She puts her finger to her mouth. "You are not supposed to talk to me." And off she goes to therapy.

3
EXPIRATION: 74 HOURS

It's impossible. I've been at it for hours, and there's just no way. I stand exactly where she was. I have a fair supply of apples collected from our apple tree. They're not edible, but they make perfectly good ammo. I pick up another one and throw it with all my might. It crashes on the lawn and rolls to join the dozen other apples that landed a gazillion miles away from the target.

I pick up another apple and take a few steps toward the angel.

Knock knock knock!

What?

Knock knock knock!

I turn toward the house. Zelda's looking at me from her window, mouthing something I can't make out. She mimes throwing the apple and then points at me.

"I can't hear you!"

She tries to open the window, but it's permanently sealed, and the glass is unbreakable. She waves at me, like *Come, come, little dwarf!*

I know it's a bad idea, but I really want to learn more about throwing apples. I climb on top of the water tank, step on the little roof above the porch, and crouch in front of her window.

"You're doing it wrong," she says. "You must hit the target first, then throw the apple and reverse time with your mind. That is the only way to bend the space between you and the artifact—you get it? It is basic psychophysics."

Nice theory, but I shrug it off. "Why don't you just admit it?"

"What?"

"That you got lucky, or that you're a total star at throwing things. Why do you always need to make up a weird story for everything?"

"You cannot bend time, Earthling? Even a little?"

"I broke Dad's watch once. Does that qualify?"

"By Zook!" She bangs her forehead against the window and closes her eyes. "This is such a primitive planet!"

———————

You must hit the target first, I repeat like a mantra. *Then throw.*

I stare intently at the jaw of the rubber T. rex on top of my desk. I think of the marble entering its mouth. *You must hit the target first*. I close my eyes, reopen them, and throw. Damn!

I knocked down Bart Simpson to the left of the T. rex.

Last marble. Sixteen throws, zero hits. I stand up from my bed. *Focus, David*. Here is the marble. There is the T. rex. I picture the marble disappearing inside its jaws.

And throw—

And shit!

"You're throwing like a Zokoplasm from planet Altar!" Zelda says from the hallway.

That's the problem with the high-tech gizmo on her ankle: Dad doesn't lock her in her room anymore, so she's free to move around the house and mock me at will. "Are you even *trying* to bend time?"

"There's no time thingy. You just got lucky. Mystery solved."

She sneers and points at the T. rex. "Give me those marbles."

———————

Twelve throws. Twelve hits.

She's so annoying! And pretty amazing, too.

She flips upside down and stands on her head on top of my bed and—*pop!*—Thirteen throws. Thirteen hits. The marble didn't touch the T. rex's teeth or anything.

"Can you teach me how to do that?"

"I do not think it is possible, Earthling. Not if you cannot bend time." She reaches for the gizmo on her ankle and starts pulling on it with both hands.

"You better be careful with that," I warn. "It goes off easily."

"You know how it works?"

"Sure." I give her another handful of marbles. "You're not the first one to have one of those here. It's unbreakable, but if you try to break it, it goes off. You leave the house, it goes off. You keep pulling on it like that, and it will *definitely* go off."

"And then?"

She rolls down from her headstand. Her legs land on mine. Physical contact! She doesn't seem bothered by it, but I stiffen up like someone just bit my ass.

"Then?"

I retract my legs carefully. "Then the policemen come and get you."

She leans over to give the gizmo a last pull. I can see some sort of tattoo at the edge of her sweater collar. She turns to me. "And then?"

Her hand lands beside mine on the bed. I can feel the heat radiating from the tips of her fingers. If she gets any closer, she'll have to sit on my lap.

"I . . ."

"What?"

"I don't know. Like . . . they put you in a proper nuthouse. You never, ever get out. Just like Dad said." Even swallowing excess saliva seems like a major accomplishment.

"What is wrong with you? Why do you make a face like a dead fish?"

Fourteen throws. Fourteen hits.

I jump off the bed and take refuge by my bookshelves, far away from her. I pretend that I need to reorganize my Fantastic Four comics, doing my best not to look like a dead fish.

"Why are you trying to get to Paris?" I ask, sorting the comics by villains: Namor, Galactus, Doctor Doom. "I realize that Cornouaille is not, like, *zee* place to find a boyfriend, but there's the city of Rouen just a few miles west. There're plenty of boys in Rouen. They drive around the high schools on their motorcycles." Apparently, the girls love that.

"I am not looking for *any* boy. I am looking for my *chosen one*," she says. "And he is in Paris."

Fifteen throws. Fifteen hits.

"How do you know that?"

"Zook told me." She rolls onto her stomach and studies the Tintin prints on my pillows and duvet. Not the sexiest choice of bedspread, I'm afraid.

"What's Zook?" I ask.

"She's the one watching over me and all Vahalalians. What you Earthlings call God."

Even the Silver Surfer on the cover of the comic I'm holding looks shocked.

"You talk to God?"

"Yes."

Sixteen throws. Sixteen hits.

"And *God* told you your future boyfriend is in Paris?"

"Yes."

This girl is nuts, the Silver Surfer seems to agree right before I return him to his place on the shelf.

"Did *God* tell you his name?" I ask ultra slowly, keeping in mind that I'm talking to a seriously deranged girl.

"No." She turns to me and throws the last marble without even looking. "But Zook told me the only important thing about him."

"What?"

"His entire genetic code," she says, yawning.

How romantic!

"Are we done?" she asks, standing up and stretching like she wants to leave.

"Wait!" I don't want her to leave now. I want to hear more of her crazy stories. And maybe watch her throw another set of marbles. "We've established that you talk to God. Not bad. But . . . do you have any other powers?"

"Powers?"

I grab a random Fantastic Four comic, *The Coming of Galactus!*, and hand it to her to illustrate my point. She flips through the pages, narrowing her eyes and trying to make sense of it.

"You know. Flying. Self-combusting. Turning into a rubber band. Things you do on your girl planet that we can't do around here. Superpowers."

"I do not know where to start." She makes a face, like she can think of a gazillion things, just off the top of her head.

"Like what?"

"Space Splash."

"Space Splash!" I start laughing but immediately stop when her green eyes go two notches meaner. "Okay, what's Space Splash?"

"The ability to be at two points in space at the same time, making us able to move fast."

"How fast? Like a plane?"

"Faster than anything you know. Our martial art is based on Space Splashing."

Can't wait to see some of that. "Show me!"

She shakes her head and hands me the comic. "I cannot, Earthling."

"You *cannot*?" Oh, what a surprise! I smile, returning *The Coming of Galactus!* to the brand-new Galactus section.

"It would kill me if I tried, because of Space Flop."

"Sure. Space Flop." I wish she could hear herself.

"Traveling a very long distance in space causes Space Flop. When I am no longer Space Flopped, I can Space Splash."

A serious Marvel guy like me prefers more complex scenarios. "Space Flop. Space Splash. I'm Space Shocked!" I laugh.

"Do not mock me!" she barks. "Do you think I would be trapped here if I could Space Splash? When Space Flop is over, an army of Earthlings will not be able to stop me."

She squashes Tintin's face on the pillow with her fist and looks at me like I'm next.

Which reminds me:

1. Do not laugh at a patient's bonkersness.

2. Do not upset someone who regularly breaks people's bones.

"I get it. You're flopped. When you're not, you'll splash. Don't . . . *flip* on me. Hot cocoa?" I try to walk away. Cocoa should restore the peace between us.

She leaps right in front of me, grabs my T-shirt, and pulls me toward her till I can feel her . . . well, *bazongas* right there against my chest. "I could punch you in the nose and give you a taste of Space Splashing," she says, raising a threatening fist.

I've never been this close to a girl before. And if I weren't so scared about the aforementioned punch, I would think she smells amazing! Like honey and . . . *space spices*?

"Ahem!"

We turn around. She lets go of me. Dad is standing in the hall, looking annoyed and probably wondering what part of "leave Zelda alone" I didn't get.

"A word, please," he says, motioning for me to follow him into the hall.

I'm totally going to get it, Dad's way: a long lecture on the importance of keeping promises, and I'll probably have to read a book on the subject, too.

Dad's lying in bed reading his own article, which was recently published in a scientific journal, as if to remind himself of his own principles of inner peace and tolerance before Mom arrives tomorrow morning to pick me up and give him hell.

I'm lying beside him, thinking of Zelda and pretending to read the copy of *Sophie's World* he gave me at the beginning of summer.

Dad wants to make sure there's no more interaction between me and Zelda, so I'm sleeping in his room tonight, which is a real bummer, since Dad snores like a jet engine and I'm dying for more *interaction*.

"If you knew someone's DNA," I ask suddenly, "could you tell for sure that you were meant to be together?"

"Well . . ." Dad drops the journal on his lap and thinks about it. "It's quite a theory she's got there. If only it were that simple!"

"How do you know, then?"

"It's more a question of trial and error."

Like him and Mom, if you put the emphasis on *error*.

"But if it's not DNA, there must be *something* that makes you want to be with someone."

"I guess love would be that something."

Love! Now, that's a fishy subject, I tell you.

"Did you tell Zelda that?" I ask.

"I did, actually." Dad switches off his bedside light.

I put my own book away and switch off my light, too. "What did she say?"

"She said love was a sin."

Sweet dreams.

4

EXPIRATION: 62 HOURS

I'm having a nightmare where Zelda orders the T. rex to eat me when I'm woken up by Dad's voice. I switch on the light, get out of bed, and find him pacing the kitchen in his pajamas, talking on his cell phone and scratching his bald head hysterically.

"I don't know how she did it!" he keeps repeating. "I've never seen anything like this in my entire life! It's shocking! Unbelievable!"

I shoot to the staircase and run toward Zelda's room.

"David!" Dad calls after me and makes gestures, like, *Wait a second, don't go in her room*, etc., but I shrug and pretend I don't understand, and he's way too busy on the phone to stop me.

"Zelda?" I call.

I go into her room. "Zel . . ."

Her gizmo lies in the middle of the room, intact, unbroken, perfectly closed, but there's no Zelda in it. I hear Dad's heavy footsteps. He stops beside me. We contemplate the gizmo for a while.

"She's gone again," he says, looking like he ate a slug and it refuses to slide down.

———————————

A bald policeman inspects the gizmo from every angle and passes it to his hairier colleague. "Have you ever seen anyone take one of these off?" he asks.

"Not without breaking it or setting it off," Dad answers, serving them coffee.

They're plainclothes officers. The uniformed ones are outside, confiscating pitchforks and trying to calm down the Cornouaillois enraged by the news of this third escape.

"How do you think she did it?" The policeman puts the gizmo down in the middle of the kitchen table.

Dad sighs and scratches his chin. "She would have had to . . . well, hmm . . ."

He has absolutely no idea.

They drink their coffee while staring at the mysterious gizmo. I'm having cold milk. It's breakfast time. There are croissants on the table, but no one really has any appetite.

"Maybe she managed to open it, take it off, and lock it back real fast before the alarm went off," suggests one of the policemen.

They think about it and then shake their heads unanimously.

"This is *nuts*!" the bald policeman says, blowing on his coffee.

"Nothing is ever . . . nuts," Dad mumbles unconvincingly.

There's a strangely silent gizmo and a girl who vanished into thin air to prove him wrong.

"Go get dressed," Dad says, realizing I'm still wearing my old Tintin pajamas (more evidence of Dad's fascination for the guy). "Your mother will be mad if you're not ready when she arrives."

He's wrong about that. Mom will get mad no matter what. And anyway it's already too late: We can hear her car roaring up the gravel path.

I hesitantly walk out and stop in front of the garage to welcome her and see if she ran over any villagers who got in her way. Her fancy Mercedes sport coupe slides to a halt just an inch away from me. Mom gets out, blowing cigarette smoke through her nose, dragon style.

She's wearing the size-two black ensemble she uses for work. Black sunglasses. Black hair tightly pulled back. She looks like the Angel of Death on a business trip. Even the Cornouaillois stop yelling, sensing danger.

"Do you really think I have nothing better to do than come here?" she says. That's her version of *Hi, darling—how have you been?* "I'm missing a court appointment for you."

Mom's a divorce lawyer. She's brilliant at it.

"Hi, Mom," I say carefully.

She takes off her sunglasses. She's even scarier when you can see her cold blue eyes. "How can you let him dress you like this?" she coughs out. She's not a big Tintin fan, either. And she is very particular about how I dress, even to go to bed. She wants me to make her look chic at any time of day or night, just like any of her other fashion accessories.

Dad comes out of the house to defend his choice of pajamas.

"You!" Mom barks, pointing at him like a wound-up wrestler about to trash him around the ring. "You're going to pay for this!"

"I know," Dad says, avoiding eye contact.

He's a strong man normally, but when Mom's around, he has the personality of a bathroom rug.

"And you!" she barks at me. "Go get dressed and then wait for me in the car while I deal with your father."

Five minutes later, I'm dressed, packed, and waiting in the car, already slightly sick from the cigarette stench. "Can I say good-bye to Dad?" I ask when Mom joins me.

"No." She starts the engine and reverses at high speed. The policemen hardly have time to push the villagers out of her way. She drives over the foot of Monsieur Dupuis, the mayor of Cornouaille and Dad's nemesis.

"Losers," Mom says, lighting a cigarette and speeding away, ignoring the agonized screams.

I guess there's really no point telling Mom about Zelda's miraculous escape. It's not only that she's too busy yelling at her assistant over the phone—it's that she wouldn't care, period. If something's not about her, Édouard (her longtime partner), or one of her divorce cases, she doesn't want to hear about it.

———————

Mom has a thing for sports cars, chain-smoking menthol cigarettes, swearing, and giving truck drivers the finger as she passes them on the highway.

The combination always makes me nauseous, but I'd never say so. Mom can't stand for me to show any signs of weakness, and she hates when I get sick.

"AHOW!"

"What now?" Mom asks, blowing a toxic cloud at me.

"Nothing."

"So why are you howling?"

Actually, it wasn't me howling after Mom swerved like a mad-woman to pass yet another truck. It came from behind the tiny backseat—right where the trunk is.

"What's wrong with you?" She squeezes my cheeks in her cold hand and inspects my face. "You've turned all green. You're not going to be sick, are you?!"

"I . . . I'm . . . nothing."

"Don't you dare vomit in my car! I just had it cleaned."

———————

Mom's swearing like a sailor because we're stuck in a traffic jam trying to get into Paris. I can't stop thinking about what's inside the trunk. Mom picks up her cell phone and calls Édouard. He was her business partner before he became her lover and the reason she left Dad. He's an okay guy, I guess. Unlike Dad, he can handle Mom's bad temper, and they're always yelling at each other like it's a lifestyle.

She starts yelling at him as soon as he picks up the phone: This! That! And every freaking thing in between! One way or another, we all exist to irritate her. The only time Mom doesn't yell at him—or me—is on Sundays, right after we all have an afternoon nap. Then she becomes very cuddly and sweet for an hour or two. The rest of the time, she's a demon.

An hour later, Mom runs out of cigarettes, and we're still stuck on the highway. She moans like she just realized her liver's missing.

She phones Édouard and starts yelling at him again, this time adding the missing cigarettes to her long list of frustrations. He should understand. He's a heavy smoker, too. Whenever they're both at home, I have to lock myself in my room, stuff toilet paper in the keyhole, and open all the windows—even in the middle of winter—just so I can breathe.

Which reminds me: Don't you need to punch holes in a trunk for someone to breathe inside?

Mom is near hysterical when she double-parks in front of the tobacco shop by our apartment. She jumps out of the car like her seat is on fire.

I really pray she never tries to quit smoking—or if she does, I want at least an ocean between us.

"Zelda! It's me, David. We're in Paris," I say, turning to the backseat.

Nothing. Not a word, not a movement.

"Are you back there? In the trunk? Can you breathe?"

Still no sign of life.

"You can talk to me. I won't tell Mom or anyone if you're in the trunk. I mean Mom would just freak out, and we don't want that, trust me. And I'm like Dad—I don't want them to put you in prison. Zelda!"

Maybe I was wrong. Maybe Zelda was never in the car.

"If you're in the trunk, I want to tell you, everybody is really impressed with you. Like, the policemen—they looked like they'd swallowed a fly when they saw the gizmo. Did you really open it and close it really fast? That's the best theory they came up with."

"Are you going to shut up, Earthling?" Zelda shouts from inside the trunk.

I knew it!

"Idiots!" Mom yells, getting back in the car. She slams the door and drops a pack of menthol cigarettes and a pile of women's magazines on my lap.

"Everybody is driving me *crazy* today." She lights a menthol and blows the smoke in my face. "What's with you?"

"Nothing."

"Then stop looking at me like that. You remind me of your father."

Never a good thing.

Our apartment is perfect. Mom keeps it this way, and if you move or touch *anything*, you are positively dead. If Dad lives in the middle of nowhere, Mom lives right in the center of the world—which happens to be in the middle of Paris, across the street from the Jardin du Luxembourg in Saint Germain.

The apartment is huge, and every wall is covered with expensive modern art and antiques. As far as I can tell, Mom earns tons of money.

I drop my bag in my room. I'm so nervous, I don't even care that Mom has redecorated it into a designer minimalist white nightmare without even telling me. I need to get back to the car and free Zelda from the trunk.

"You like it?" Mom asks, passing by.

"I—"

"Try not to touch or move anything. And leave the pillows exactly where they are. The man who arranged them is an artist."

I look around. One item is dramatically missing: my fish tank and its occupant, Pixel, my beloved goldfish.

"Where's Pixel?"

"He died."

She fluffs up the pillows and then uses her finger to collect a single speck of dust from a bookshelf, totally avoiding looking at my pained face.

"Mom? Did you flush him down the toilet?"

She'd threatened to flush Pixel down the toilet many times in the past.

She sighs. "I gave him to the doorman. The aquarium didn't fit the new design. But I got you a new computer." She nods toward a brand-new white iMac on top of my brand-new shiny white desk.

"There's money on the kitchen table for your lunch," she says, taking a last Polaroid look at my room. "If you move anything . . .," she warns, and off she goes, power walking all the way down to her office on the Île de la Cité.

Mom loves power walking. It's the only way she can smoke and work out at the same time, since "those idiots" at her gym won't let her smoke on the treadmill.

I run down the stairs rather than waiting for the elevator, flash the magnetic card at the security doors, and run to Mom's car. The alarm is going wild, God knows for how long, and I frantically press the remote to put an end to it. The car whines a last annoyed *bip-bip*, and the racket stops. Now all you can hear is Zelda hissing, puffing, and trying to shoulder her way out of the trunk.

"I'm here!" I say, and open it for her.

There are a few divorce case files on one side and a half-empty bottle of Evian water on the other. And there's Zelda in the middle, looking at me like she could bite.

"What took you so long?" she yells, springing out of the trunk like a pissed-off jack-in-the-box.

5

EXPIRATION: 58 HOURS

Zelda is very pale, and she's dirty and muddy like she's been hiding in a hole in the ground. She looks like the living dead with a bad hangover, and I'm praying that the doorman was too busy feeding his new friend Pixel to see us getting into the elevator.

She moans as she falls onto my new designer-white futon—and to be perfectly honest, it doesn't look very comfortable.

"Water," she barks.

I run into my bathroom and fill up my toothbrush tumbler. Our hands touch when I pass her the glass, and I can feel she's burning hot.

"What's wrong with you?"

"I Space Splashed out of the gizmo. I was not ready. I was still Space Flopped."

"Are you going to be okay?"

She clutches her stomach with both hands and lies on her side. "No. I'm not going to be *okay*, Earthling. My inner organs are going to melt, and I'm probably going to die."

Dying is a serious condition. I kneel in front of her and instinctively try to touch her forehead to check if she really has a fever. *ZAP!* She grabs my hand just before I manage to touch her.

"What are you doing?"

"I was just trying to—oooouch!"

If she squeezes my hand any harder, she's going to break a finger.

"Don't you ever try to touch me again. Understood?"

"Yes, yes, YEESS!" I manage to scream right before she squashes my hand into a pulp.

She releases it.

I walk away, shaking my hand and blowing on my fingers. "I was just trying to check if you had fever and needed to see a doctor."

"I don't need a doctor. I *am* a doctor."

This girl is full of surprises.

———————

Zelda has a peculiar way of practicing medicine. She calls it *acoustic therapy*, and shockingly, it's pretty much what a lunatic would do to fix a medical problem: sing an alien lullaby to her belly button.

"Stop watching me like that, dwarf," she complains. "You're distracting me, and I cannot hit the anesthetic notes."

She goes back to her strange wordless melody, sounding very much like a whale at singing practice.

"Can I just say one thing?"

She shakes her head. "If you speak, it will not work. You have a particularly annoying voice."

"I think you have a high fever, Zelda." I nearly lost my right hand trying to confirm that.

"I know." She lifts her sweater and starts caressing her stomach. "That is what I am fixing."

I have my doubts about acoustic therapy, but one thing's for sure: She has incredible abs—and they're covered in very sexy tattoos.

"Mom keeps tons of medicine in her bathroom," I say. "Don't you want an aspirin? She also takes this blue pill that turns her into a happy babbling jellyfish whenever she has a migraine."

Zelda stops caressing her stomach and looks up at me with tired, feverish eyes.

"Your medicine is prehistoric. You have not discovered life energy, and you are thousands of years away from acoustic therapy." And with that said, she goes back to singing to her belly button.

————

"The fever is almost gone," she says after sleeping for about an hour on the futon.

I have no way to confirm that, and I'm not about to try to touch her again. I prepared ham and cheese sandwiches and a milkshake with strawberry syrup and a few drops of vanilla extract. I lay the tray beside the futon. "Try the milkshake."

She takes the glass hesitantly. She's going to love it. I got the recipe from the Disney Channel years ago—it's a real killer.

"It's not poison. Milk is good for the stomach."

She smiles, like I've said something particularly naive. It's the first time I've seen her smile. She gets these cute little wrinkles on the sides of her lips.

She drinks my milkshake. "Thank you."

We might be a "primitive planet," like she said, but some of us have an advanced sense of hospitality.

She sighs and puts down the milkshake. "I'm cured!" she decides.

She's good—she fixed an imaginary illness with an imaginary therapy in, like, no time.

She stands up, stretches, and moves on to the next problem: "Clothes. Quick." She shoots straight for Mom's room.

"You don't need to go in there," I say, trying to stop her from reaching Mom's ultrarestricted walk-in closet. "You can have any of my clothes instead."

"Don't be absurd. You are half my size."

She can be so harsh sometimes!

I freeze and gasp. She has dropped her oversize jeans in the middle of Mom's room, and now she's peeling off her sweater. I look away and turn around, like watching the pigeons outside the window is way more interesting than looking at her getting naked. "Zelda! Please, put something on! I mean . . . unless it looks too expensive."

Mom has a standard punishment for anyone touching her beloved designer clothing: death.

"By Zook! I found proper clothing, Earthling!"

I hear her shuffling things around in the closet and then sliding into something, *slip slap slop!* Whatever she found, it sounds like it's made of rubber.

"Turn around," she orders.

Okay. I turn around carefully. Ta-da! I look briefly and blush like a tomato in spring.

Four things:

1. Zelda has no modesty whatsoever.

2. She has many more tribal tattoos than I could ever imagine. Her upper legs, arms, shoulders—no part of her body has been spared.

3. She's wearing Mom's teeny-weeny black Speedo bikini, the one Mom uses to show how fit and trim she is. Édouard has a name for it: Outrageous.

4. Power Girl has *nothing* on her!

"This is exactly what we wear in Vahalal," she says happily.

"You mean this is how you dress to . . . walk around in public?"

"Of course."

"Zelda. That is a swimsuit. On Earth, women wear them to . . . swim or . . ." I can't think of any other reason to wear Mom's Outrageous Speedo. "Put *that thing* back where you found it. I'll get you a clean sweater and a fresh pair of comfy jeans. Okay?"

She's not even listening to me. She's already moving to the deep end of the closet where Mom stores her gigantic collection of high boots and dangerous stilettos. "I need something of the highest quality. Tough, flexible, protective, and comfortable for combat."

That definitely sounds like most of Mom's footwear. She chooses a pair of knee-high leather boots, then sits on the floor and zips one on. *Ziiiiiiip*.

"Where'd you get all those tattoos?" I say, looking at the ones on her back.

"Tattoos?"

"The drawings all over your body."

"They are not drawings," she says, zipping up the second boot. *Ziiiiiiip*. "They are biological markings that show who I am and what I have done." She stands up to show me a tattoo on the inside of her left arm, a symbol that looks like a six-legged ant on steroids. "This one, for example, proves that I am a Vahalalian." She shows me another one on the inside of her thigh. "This one recalls my exploits during the Unholy Wars. Each of the lines represents a sinner I slaughtered." She moves the Speedo just slightly. "Here, that is the Battle of Loki. See it?" She shows me the tattoo on the base of her . . . well, left bazoom, and *poof*, half the neurons in my head explode.

"Do you still doubt me?" she says, readjusting her bikini top.

I manage to stop staring at the Battle of Loki and look up to her eyes, shaking my head numbly. No. I don't doubt it anymore: This girl is another level of nuts.

———————

"Please, not that vase! It's a Philippe Starck. It's worth a fortune."

"I need it. Look." She measures it against her arm. "It will make a perfect arm shield."

"Mom adores it. Please put it down."

I make a move to take it back. She grabs the neck of my T-shirt and holds me at a safe distance, coolly examining the vase from different angles. She touches it with the tip of her tongue. "Is it carbon based?" she asks, like she could *taste* that.

"It's fiberglass and wood. Very unique. Give it back." I desperately try to reach for it, but she has such long, strong arms. "Please."

"If I break the wood off . . ."

Break is such a cruel word. "Choose something else! We can cut some cardboard and paint it."

"I need this artifact."

"It's *art*!"

"What you Earthlings call art is useless. Weapons and shields are necessary."

It's a tough universe out there.

She lifts the vase above her head and then slams it against the wall. *Clunk!*

"Noooo!"

There's no reasoning with this girl. She has broken Mom's vase in two and now slides her arm into the fiberglass part, looking very pleased with herself.

We're so busted! "Mom will kill both of us for this."

"No. She will just kill *you*. Good-bye and good luck, Earthling," she says, shooting toward the door with nothing on but a tiny bikini, knee-high leather boots, and a broken vase around her left arm.

"You can't possibly go out dressed like that."

"Why not?"

"This is France! You're practically naked. You're going to start a riot! Please!"

She sighs, grabs a black coat hanging in the foyer, and buttons it over the swimsuit. "Are you happy now?"

"No!" She's chosen Mom's absolute favorite summer coat. "That's a Lagerfeld!"

But Zelda doesn't care. She opens the door, pausing in front of the mirror to inspect her reflection, and then grabs Mom's vintage Cardin sunglasses to complete her outfit.

"You *cannot* take those glasses," I say with a trembling voice. "Mom would rather give *me* away than see those gone."

"Your problem." Zelda shrugs. "I must go find my chosen one. Good-bye, dwarf."

I follow her to the staircase. "You're going to bring the coat back, aren't you?"

———

"Stop following me!" she says as she crosses the road toward the park.

"Mom really loves that coat. Seriously. It means the world to her."

And the sunglasses! There're, like, five pairs of them left in the entire world, and those were given to Mom by one of her clients as a token of his appreciation for getting him divorced so quickly. Mom adores those glasses.

"Okay, dwarf. Take the coat back and leave me alone."

She's about to take it off. It's one o'clock. The Jardin du Luxembourg is crowded with people on their lunch breaks, kids going to the pond with their miniature sailboats, old people feeding pigeons. She's about to show them all her tattoos—or biological markings or *whatever* they are—and create a scandal.

"Keep the coat on!"

"Not if you keep following me. *What is wrong with you?*"

I don't know. She's bonkers, no doubt. Way more than anyone Dad ever fixed, even that poor boy who thought he was three people at the same time. But . . . I'm . . . I just . . . I want to . . . to *be* with her, very badly. "I can be useful."

"I doubt it."

"I know this city inside out. I know . . . *Earthlings*. I'm able to talk to them without smashing anything on their heads. I . . . I'm very good with maps! Er . . . there are so many ways I can help you. I can be, like, your . . . *guide*."

She takes off Mom's sunglasses and stares right into my eyes. She looks a bit scary. "Are you offering to become my Pudin?"

"What's a Pudding?"

"A Pudin: a lower life-form renouncing its freedom to serve a Traveler."

"Oh. You mean like . . . *a slave*?"

"Exactly, Earthling."

Slave sounds bad. Still, it's better than "that miserable guy she abandoned in the middle of the park."

"Sure," I say. "I can be your Pudding or Pudin or . . . anything!" As long as she lets me stay with her.

"Good." She puts both hands on my shoulders and starts making noises like a dolphin: *Quikidizikzik taaak taaak!*

"What was that?" Does she want fish?

"I swore you in. You are now officially my Pudin and will serve me until you die or until I leave this planet." And—*zoom*—she walks away at high speed.

"Where are you going?" I call after her.

"To the Temple of Zook, Pudin."

I love it when she calls me that.

"Zook? Your goddess? Here in Paris?"

"There's a Temple of Zook in every major city in the universe."

"Oh, but of course!"

She stops. "Are you mocking me again, Pudin?"

I might have laughed a little. "Sorry."

"Do you realize what being a Pudin means?"

"I guess we're like Don Quixote and Sancho Panza. I'm Sancho."

"Who?"

"Never mind. Let's go fight some windmills."

6
EXPIRATION: 55 HOURS

I always wondered what was behind the medieval walls of some of the oldest palaces in Le Marais.

According to Zelda: an extraterrestrial temple built to the glory of Zook, goddess of the Vahalalians.

"This is it," Zelda says, nodding toward an ancient chapel squeezed between two tall buildings at the end of a dark courtyard off the tiny rue des Oiseaux.

It's not the futuristic metal-and-glass construction I imagined it would be. It's more like any other old Gothic church in Paris—if darker, smaller, and yes, somehow scarier.

Zelda pushes the old wooden door. There's no lock, no chains, but then again, there's nothing to steal. A few wooden benches, a few burning candles giving off the only light to see by, bare stone walls, and a fading depiction of the Virgin Mary painted on the back wall behind the altar.

"Are you sure this is the place?" I point at the painting. "This is a painting of the Virgin Mary. And she's *very* Catholic."

"This is not *Mary*. This is *Zook*."

Oh, sorry—my mistake!

"And this is not a painting, it is a door."

"A door?" I approach the painting and knock on it. *Bonk bonk bonk!* It's stone hard. "Is there a secret passage behind it?"

"You could say that."

There is some sort of pit at the base of the painting, like someone actually tried to dig his way to the other side. "Is the real temple behind this wall?"

"No, this is the temple."

"So what's behind the wall, then?"

"You see the star Zook is pointing at, the one right above her head?"

That's right. Mary—I mean, Zook—is pointing two fingers at a fading white spot right above her head.

"That is my sun."

"Okay. . . ."

"Do you understand?"

"No."

She puts it in plain words for me: "Whoever walks through this wall will travel back to Vahalal."

"You mean . . . this is a freaking STARGATE?" I laugh again. Oops.

She gives me a dark look.

"It's just funny because of the show. You know with the . . ." I try to draw a door with my hands and pantomime opening it. "And then—*zoom*—into a wormhole. Right?" At least I know where she gets all her ideas from: TV!

She sighs. I'm such a disappointing Pudin.

"Zelda, I don't want to ruin your *thing*. But this is a stone wall." I slap the Virgin Mary's stomach. It's hard, cold, and painful on my hand.

"It looks like a wall because it is locked," she explains, squatting behind the altar. "But like every door, it has a key."

"And you have that key?"

"Yes." She puts her hand inside a large crack at the base of the altar and pulls out a small metal box.

"Is that the key?"

"No, this is not the key. It is a few items I brought from Vahalal."

Like an essential interstellar travel pack.

"There," she says, lifting the sleeve of Mom's coat and showing me a tattoo that looks like a strange triangular octopus proudly holding a stick.

"There what?"

"That, Pudin, is the key. Whoever carries this marking can walk through the door." She caresses it gently. "I don't have much time left. Look. It's already fading."

It does look lighter than her other tattoos, like a cheap homemade one she got years ago.

"In a few days, the key will expire. If I don't find my chosen one before that, I'll be trapped on this ridiculous planet forever."

"Oh. That would be *awful*."

She sighs, totally missing the irony in my voice. She puts her hands on my shoulders. "Many Travelers have come here and failed." She squeezes my shoulders till it hurts. "But we're going to find him or die trying. Won't we, Pudin?"

I nod. Sure thing. Dying should totally be part of my job description.

She stops mauling me and lets go. "Good Pudin."

"Okay, let me get this straight." I rub my shoulders. "Because you have that weird octopus thing on your arm, you could just . . . walk through this wall and, *zoooof*, shoot back to your planet right before my eyes?"

"It's not an octopus. It's a key. And no, Earthling. I won't open the door." She kneels in front of the painting. "My chosen one will, once I give him the key." She touches her goddess's feet in a sign of obedience. "And then together we will fly through space and back to my planet."

"You're taking *him* back with you?" My voice gets a few notches higher with surprise.

She turns away from Zook and stands up. "That is what we do, Earthling: We give them the key and take them back to Vahalal, lock them in the Tower of Tor, and make sure they never escape."

It gets worse for the poor chosen one by the second. "You want to give the guy a piece of your own skin and lock him up in a prison?!"

"The Tower of Tor is not a prison. It's more like . . . what you Earthlings call a zoo. And I won't give him a piece of my skin. I will transfer the key to him during sexual intercourse. Are you all right, Pudin? You appear to be emotionally disturbed."

"I'm fine." Except all the blood in my body rushed to my face the second she said *sexual intercourse*.

It's windy over the Seine River. We're crossing the Pont Notre-Dame, going back to the Rive Gauche. I'm thinking about the painting of Zook, the door to Vahalal, the Tower of Tor, the key octopus tattoo thingy on her arm. But mostly, I must confess, I'm thinking of Zelda . . . well . . . removing her Speedo and *transferring* the key to her chosen one. I feel dizzy. And a bit scared. I wonder if I should phone Dad immediately and have the cuckoo squad come pick her up with their butterfly nets and tranquilizer darts, because if she believes any or all of these things she's talking about, I've become the Pudin of one seriously deranged girl. But I just can't resist her. She's the most interesting person I've ever met. The most . . . I don't know. Special.

She stops right in the middle of the bridge and takes off Mom's sunglasses to take a better look at my city. "He is out there somewhere," she says. "And I will find him."

Oh God, I'm so confused I could scream. The wind plays with her long hair, most of it landing over her face. She's so damn beautiful.

"Zelda?"'

"Yes, Pudin?"

"People on Earth don't walk around spelling out their DNA."

"I know that, Pudin. I've been studying your primitive civilization."

"My point is, that's not how we find a, you know, girlfriend or boyfriend or whatever."

"Not boyfriend, chosen one."

"What I'm saying . . . it might come as a surprise to you, but if all you know is his DNA, it's going to be really hard to find him. Probably impossible."

And then, out of nowhere, she grabs my face and kisses me. Her lips part. Her tongue touches mine.

Olivier was wrong. This isn't anything like raw chicken at all. It's more like *spinning* and *falling*.

I close my eyes and clumsily put my arms around her to make sure we'll stay like this forever.

It's the first time I've ever kissed a girl.

I'm kissing a girl.

I. AM. KISSING. A. GIRL. Until—*zoom*—she abruptly pushes me away and all the happiness drains out of me.

I open my eyes. "Did I . . . ? Was I . . . ? Did you . . . ?" But, more importantly, "Why did you do that?" You should hear the high pitch of my voice.

"To show you how it works."

"What?!"

"Travelers are experts in gustative biochemistry. That is how we sample someone's DNA. By the way, you are not a match."

Sometimes her little Spacegirl fantasy totally sucks.

———————

"Why are you emotionally disturbed again?" she asks, trying to keep up with me as we pass Saint-Eustache Cathedral. "Pudin, stop running away from me!"

"I'm not emotionally anything!" But I am running away from her. I just don't feel like playing her little games anymore.

I stop and turn around to face her. "I don't think you're funny!"

"I am not meant to be funny."

Apparently.

"Are you upset about me sampling you negative?"

"Oh, so shoving your tongue inside my mouth is called 'sampling me negative'?"

"It is the most reliable way to determine who is my chosen one and who is not." (I.e., me.)

"That's that, then? You're going to kiss every boy, man, and grandpa in Paris? That's . . . very unhygienic, Zelda." I tap my head. "You might want to change your story a bit and just pretend you carry around a picture of the lucky guy."

"I do have pictures of him," she says, opening the metal box she got from the altar and retrieving a small booklet from it. "But face recognition is only seventy percent accurate. Sampling is ninety-nine percent accurate."

Sigh. "I don't know what's more annoying. That you believe all this crap or that you're just playing me."

"I am not *playing* you, Pudin. Lying is a sin."

She takes my hand and slams the booklet into it. "There. That is he. Take a look."

I open it. It's a collection of credit-card-sized pictures printed directly on metal. Let's see. He's . . . omifreakinggod!

"See, you do not look like him at all. I just sampled you as a matter of illustration."

"This is a joke, right?" I ask, looking at the first picture.

"What do you mean?"

I turn the cards, slowly at first and then faster and faster. I look up, waiting for her to break into a laugh and say "Of course this is a joke. Now let's do something different, like rob a bank."

"You're going to tell me you have no idea who this is?" I show her the last picture in the booklet.

"That's the Earthling I came for. My chosen one. His image was reconstructed based on his exact genetic code."

————————

All the way to the Internet café, I think, she's not nuts at all, she's just nasty, and she's been playing me the whole time.

I sit her in front of a computer. I open Google. I choose the images search. I type the name. I hit Enter and get 2,990,000 results. I turn to her. Her eyes widen.

"See anyone familiar?" I ask.

"It is *him*," she says, pointing at the screen, her eyes getting wider and greener.

"Oh, stop the act." I click on a picture where he's not dressed like Jack Sparrow, a nice black-and-white picture from when he was younger. "Is that the guy you're looking for?"

"I must kiss him to be sure."

"Ha! Kiss him! Sure!"

Zelda is just like any other girl on earth.

She wants what they all want. She wants JOHNNY DEPP!

7

EXPIRATION: 54 HOURS

"Let me just say it out loud so we can laugh together: You're going to find Johnny Depp, take him back to Vahalal, and put him in a zoo?"

"Who?"

"Him, him, him!" I yell, hysterically pointing at the computer screen. The other customers in the café turn to see what bit me.

"He looks . . . exactly like the one I am looking for. I told you, I need to—"

"Kiss him! Good luck with that, and good-bye!"

I don't even bother to log off. I drop two euros on the counter and head for the door. I've had enough. I'm going home. I'm going back to my life the way it was before she came to Cornouaille.

Johnny Depp?! Come on!

"Pudin!" She runs after me in the street. "Stop!"

She catches up with me and grabs my wrist.

"You must obey me. Disobeying a Traveler is a sin, Pudin."

"I quit!" I'm her Pudin no more.

"You cannot quit."

"Watch me!"

"What's the matter with you?" She tightens her grip on my wrist till it hurts.

"You walk around in a swimsuit. You say you're from space. And now you want to take Johnny Depp to a galaxy far, far away! Ding-dong! Doctor Schweitzer, we have reached our conclusion: You're an act, and you think I'm a fool. Period."

But she's not listening to me. She looks straight into my eyes with a weird intensity and sighs. "By Zook, I don't believe it."

"Don't believe what?"

"I have no time for this, Pudin."

"No time for what?"

"Eol-69," she says, shaking her head and looking very frustrated. "What?"

"Show me your tongue."

"Are you kissing me again?"

She sighs, grabs my hair, pulls it back, and squeezes my cheeks until I open my mouth. But she doesn't kiss me. She just studies my tongue carefully.

"I need to sing to you. Urgently. And we must find some stones."

"I'm not interested in your crazy fantasy anymore."

"Fine," she says calmly. "If I don't do anything, you'll be dead in an hour. Considering I don't have much time to spare saving your life, your sacrifice will be much appreciated."

Oh.

I *do* feel slightly light-headed suddenly. My legs give out. *Poof.* I land on my ass on the pavement. It's like all the energy is being drained out of my body. "Zelda . . . I don't feel too good. I think I need your help."

She sneers. "I knew making you my Pudin was a bad idea." And with that, she pulls me up, puts my arm over her shoulders and hers around my waist, and helps me walk.

Everything starts to spin around me. I turn to Zelda. She looks very beautiful and very focused, like she wants to be done with me quickly. "Did anyone ever tell you you're so pretty?" I mumble dizzily.

"Walk, Earthling! Delirium is a common side effect of Eol-69. And stop staring at me."

I look away. But I could swear I just made a Vahalalian blush.

————

"AAAAAAAAH!" I scream. "What happened to my eyes?!"

There are no more pupils, no more white. My eyes have turned into two shiny black balls, rolling around in terror and staring straight back at me in the bathroom mirror. I pull at my tongue. Black, black, black! Just like ink.

"I told you: Eol-69."

"What's Eol-69?!"

"It is a common bacteria on Vahalal. It is malignant to certain weaker forms of humanoids."

"Weaker?"

"Children."

Okay, now's the right time to panic. "Zelda! What's happening to me?!" I feel faint. I sit down on the toilet. Now I really wish she were just crazy. I wish Eol-69 were another of her fantasies. But look at my eyes! "What's going to happen to me?"

"Drowsiness. Paralysis, coma, and death. It is fast and painless, Pudin."

"You. Gave. Me. THIS?!"

She nods. "I suppose sampling you was not a good idea after all."

"I'm . . . sleepy."

She helps me to stand and walk into my room. I fall on my new futon. Ouch. Even when you're busy panicking and dying from an alien bug, it's impossible to ignore that this damn thing is harder than the floor.

She takes off my T-shirt. I'm so far gone, I don't even care when she unbuttons and slides off my jeans.

"Zelda?" I manage to whisper.

She hushes me and sets the stones she picked up in the Jardin du Luxembourg on my stomach. "David, I need to tell you. You are probably going to die."

Indeed. *Zoom.* I feel like I'm falling down a very large, soft hole, trying to grab something before I slide away forever. I try to reach for her hand, but my arms and legs refuse to move—paralysis! Just like she said. I've got coma and death to look forward to, then.

"If you never wake up, thank you for what you did for me," I hear her say through a billion light-years of wet cotton.

She takes my face in both hands, leans over, and sings to me.

She sings nicely. I really love . . .

————

"David?"

"Yes?"

"Are you on drugs?"

"What?"

"If you're on drugs, I will kill you."

"I'm not on drugs." I sit up. The stones fall from the bed and roll onto the floor.

Mom is standing in the middle of my room, her arms crossed tightly over her chest. "If it's not drugs, then why are you sleeping totally naked with stones on your stomach?"

"I'm not—" I look down. Oh shit! I *am* totally naked. I pull the brand-new white duvet over me and cover my eyes to hide them from her.

"My black coat was on the floor in the middle of your room. Are you dressing up in . . . *my clothes*?"

A drug addict and a cross-dresser. That's what she thinks she's dealing with.

"No. It's . . . my eyes."

She switches on the light and squats beside the futon to take a good look at her transvestite junkie son's eyes. "What about them?"

They've been contaminated by an intergalactic bug.

"They're . . . weird."

"You have my eyes, my face. They're not weird. They're beautiful." She pushes my face this way and that to examine it better. She likes my face. It reminds her of hers. "You should be thankful you didn't inherit your father's droopy features."

She looks at me intently. A normal mother would probably hug her son now. Mom's not a hugger. I'm not much of a hugger, either. I guess I got that from her, too.

She sighs, picks up the stones, and stands up. Enough bonding.

"Dinner's ready. Édouard's waiting. You know he hates waiting." She stops on her way out of the room. "Oh. By the way. Touch my coat again, and I'll give you a solid reason to take drugs." Then she abandons me, closing the door on her way out.

"Zelda?" I call.

"Here," she whispers, popping her head out of my walk-in closet. "You live, Pudin. You are stronger than I thought."

I bet she says that to all the boys.

————

I wait until Édouard and Mom disappear into their brand-new redecorated boudoir, where they will most likely yell at the TV for the rest of the evening. I gather leftover food on Mom's breakfast tray and add a carton of milk and a glass. I don't know what's with me trying to feed her milk all the time. I just picture her as a big milk lover.

She's sitting on the futon, watching the night sky through the French doors. "No stars," she remarks.

She's right. There are never any stars over Paris, just this mushy brown pollution mash.

"You shouldn't be out of the closet. And you should put some clothes on." Just imagine Mom catching her in here wearing nothing but the Speedo. Now, that would be a scene to remember.

"I should be out there looking for him."

She touches the tattoo she said was the key back to her planet. "There's so little time left." She shows me. I don't know. Maybe she's right. Maybe it does look like it's slightly fainter than the last time I saw it.

I set the tray beside her. "Did I really nearly die?"

"Yes, Earthling. You nearly died," she says, forgetting about her fading tattoo. "I sang for hours, losing precious time."

I pour her a glass of milk. My theory holds: She drinks it bottom up.

"This thing with my eyes, it really came from . . . ?" I point at the starless night sky.

She nods. She has a funny white mustache from the milk." Eol-69 is very common past Galaxy zeta-784. It is good that you did not get Eon-77."

"What does Eon-77 do?"

"You would have exploded instantly."

I look around my spotless white room. "Mom would have hated that."

We sit in front of my new iMac. Zelda's browsing through more and more pictures of Johnny Depp. Young. Older. Pirate. Pirate. Pirate. "I wish I could kiss him now," she says matter-of-factly.

"I tell you, Zelda, you're probably not the only girl thinking that right now."

"Who is that?"

She stops on a picture of him with his partner, Vanessa Paradis.

"He already has a girlfriend. He has children. He might not want to . . . *you know.*"

She shrugs. "This is not about what he wants."

Even with my door closed, we can hear Édouard and Mom going through another major argument. Zelda listens to them. A door slams. They will carry on the fight in their bedroom.

"She'd have less trouble with him if she had him neutered."

"Zelda! Don't say that word. Not in this room."

"What word?" She stands up, stretches, and yawns. It's been a long day, even for an ET.

I turn off the computer. "*Neutered.* It's sort of . . . freaky."

"Define *freaky.*"

"Well, the idea of . . ." I make a *snip-snip* motion with my fingers. "There are other ways to settle conflicts, don't you think?"

We can hear Mom yelling at the top of her lungs and then Édouard yelling back at her.

Zelda nods toward my hand. "If you knew that one of your fingers was turning you into an illogical, primitive mess and that cutting it off would make you a better person, would you hesitate?"

"A finger's, like"—I close my fist—"totally not the same thing, Zelda," I say, lying down on the bed. "You wouldn't understand. It's a guy thing."

She's too tired to keep making the case for mutilation. She lies down beside me and closes her eyes.

"You shouldn't fall asleep here," I say.

"Where should I sleep, then?"

I nod toward the closet. "Sorry. We'll make it snug."

She drags herself in. I push my sneakers aside, add some pillows, drop my sleeping bag from last year's ski camp right in the middle, and we have the perfect nest for a Spacegirl. I turn off the light.

"Why did you get emotionally disturbed?" The way she asks, it's almost a whisper. "You saw the face of my chosen one, and you became . . . *strange*."

Images flash through my mind: The kiss on Notre Dame Bridge. The very first time I saw her in Dad's office. Her face when she sang to me. Plenty of pictures of Johnny Depp.

"I don't know. I thought . . . *I don't know*."

"Emotions are bad, David. They are your weakness. You should overcome them."

I love it when she calls me David instead of dwarf, Pudin, or Earthling. But that's an emotion, right?

"If any of the symptoms of Eol-69 come back, wake me up."

I promise I will.

I can't sleep. The door to the closet is slightly open so Zelda won't die from the smell of my sneakers. I'm totally focused on the door. Imagine that. A real ET. And to think I was already obsessed with her when I thought she was just a regular loony in a supersexy swimsuit. Now I feel like my spine is connected to a high-voltage wire.

"Are you sleeping?" I call.

"No."

Silence.

"How would you rate yourself?" she asks suddenly.

"Rate myself?"

"As an Earthling, I mean."

"I . . . I never rated myself."

Silence.

"I've never treated a live male hominid before. I've done plenty of autopsies on deceased samples, of course. I normally find them utterly disgusting. The deceased ones, I mean. But some have been terribly mangled before they land on my autopsy table. The Valks can be so rough with male subjects."

Silence.

"I do not find you utterly disgusting," she says.

"Thank you," I reply hesitantly.

Silence.

"Do you like ice cream?" I ask.

"I do not know, Earthling."

"You don't know ice cream?!"

"I know exactly what ice cream is. It's a frozen food with very little nutriment and a high level of carbohydrate and fat, used by Earthlings to simulate pleasure."

I sit up on my bed. She needs to know the truth. "Zelda! Ice cream is *not* that at all!"

"I have never tried ice cream," she confesses. "Is it anything like apples?"

"Not even close," I say, jumping out of bed and slipping discreetly out of my room on a quiet expedition to the freezer.

I come back with a full pint of old-fashioned vanilla ice cream. "This, Zelda, is the greatest gift to mankind."

I switch on the light and organize an impromptu ice cream picnic on my futon. I hand her a spoon. "Try."

She brings the ice cream to the tip of her tongue, the way she always samples anything, from food to a potential boyfriend. She makes the happy face. Because this is not just ice cream. Mom buys it from überpâtissier Lenôtre. This is *zee* best ice cream in Paris and probably in the entire galaxy and beyond. Worth the interstellar trip just in itself.

"Ish cold," she says around a large spoonful.

"Ish good?"

"Ish good!"

Some things are universal. Lenôtre vanilla ice cream "ish good," no matter what planet you're from.

A pint of ice cream later, we lie side by side on my futon.

"Our northern shores are filled with giant life-forms and magnificent plants, most of them carnivorous. Someone ignorant of our ways would be killed, eaten, and digested in less than a second."

Her hands rest on her stomach, moving up and down as she breathes. She's staring up at the perfectly white ceiling and telling me all about her planet.

"Winter lasts for about two of your Earth years. There is no daylight, and electrical storms kill Vahalalians by the thousands."

I'm staring at her incredibly beautiful face while I listen.

"But spring on Vahalal is glorious," she continues. "There are more than a thousand shades of orange in our skies, and Zook is everywhere. It lasts for a very short while, then summer comes and we must hide from the sun and sulfuric storms. Sun in summer will melt you."

I'm not sure someone like Johnny Depp is going to enjoy that kind of climate.

"I wonder where he is," she says. "And how to find him."

"I was just thinking about him. All in all, you're lucky."

She stops staring at the ceiling and turns to me. She has a spot of vanilla ice cream on the side of her mouth.

"He's a celebrity," I explain. "He can run, but he cannot hide."

Her eyes! When you're this close to her, they truly look out of this world.

"What will you do if he refuses to follow you?"

She doesn't even need to think about it: "I will have to use violence."

They have a pretty peculiar definition of romance on Vahalal.

"Zelda?"

"Yes?"

"If you were to kiss me again—not that you will—but if you did, by accident or something, would I risk dying again?"

"As long as you are a child."

"I'm not a child."

"Eol-69 disagrees with you."

Damn bacteria!

"I need to sing to you a bit more." She flips around so she's sitting on top of me, and then presses down on my shoulders. "How do you feel?"

"I feel . . ." I shrug. I don't think there's a human word for what I feel with her pressed against me.

"You don't look well." She puts her hand over my heart. "Your heart beats too fast." She leans over and presses the tip of her tongue against my forehead. "I can't detect any trace of Eol-69, but your temperature is rising again."

And if she keeps licking my face like this, my blood is going to boil and my heart is going to pop.

"I'm good, I swear."

"You're not good. You're not even breathing normally." She stares at me with her amazing green eyes, her face just an inch from mine. "Are you having some kind of attack? You look all twisted."

I never thought I'd end up like this, trapped between the legs of the most fascinating girl in the world. And the most dangerous, too. Not in my wildest dreams! "I'm more than okay. I promise. I'm actually *great*!" And I mean it, too.

She shakes her head. She recognizes emotional disturbance when she sees it. "I'm going to make you sleep."

"No, wait! I don't want to sleep right now!"

Too late. She sings. I close my eyes and—*whiiiiish*—it's the end of that dream.

EXPIRATION: 37 HOURS

Daylight. Mom bursts into my room. She looks a mess. She's only vaguely wearing her bathrobe. Her eyes aren't all the way open yet, but her bad mood is already in full swing. She drops the phone on my bed. "Your father," she barks, and she's off.

She's so busy hating Dad that she doesn't even notice Zelda sleeping beside me under the duvet. She slams my door, mumbling something about idiots (her son, her ex-husband, probably Édouard, too) ruining her Saturday sleep-in.

Dad says, "I'm coming to Paris today."

"Because of Zelda?" I ask, rubbing my eyes.

"I want to be around when they catch her."

"Who's *they*?"

"I just spoke with the prosecutor in charge of her case. He talks like she's a menace to society. He's a zealous idiot who wants to make the headlines."

I've never heard Dad call anyone an idiot before—the prosecutor must be a real special breed.

"I just wish I knew where she was," Dad says.

Actually, she's getting out of my bed, yawning, stretching, adjusting the Speedo, and disappearing into my bathroom. That's where she is.

Mom and Édouard are heading to their Saturday morning brunch. I'm not invited. It's not like they're going to let me ruin their very first weekend of July plans.

"Daaaaavid! My ice cream!" Mom screams from the kitchen. I hear her slamming the freezer door. When she comes out of the kitchen, her lips are so tight they've turned blue.

"What did I tell you about my ice cream?!"

"Not to eat it," I answer carefully.

"And?"

"I ate it."

"It's not such a big deal," Édouard says, trying to appease her, the fool!

She pinches my cheek hard and shakes it. "You're going to get fat. Is that what you want?"

Mom hates fat on anyone. You should see the portions she gives Édouard. The poor guy's always starving.

"I'd rather have you dead than fat!" She actually laughs. *Yak yak yak!* That's her idea of humor. Then she slams the door, leaving me alone in the corridor.

"Zelda!" I call, going back into my room.

Where is she?

"Zellldaaa!"

"Here." She hops out of Mom's room. She's swapped the Speedo for a silver, white, and metal vintage Paco Rabanne swimsuit that Mom bought for *mucho, mucho monedo* at an auction.

She browses from one page to the next on my iMac like she can read a full tabloid article in a nanosecond.

"This is useless, Earthling! I'm losing precious time!"

She's right. It's incredible, but it's very hard to find a Web page that will help you whisk Johnny Depp away to another solar system.

"Enough!" She pushes away the mouse, stands up, and roars. She's not a big fan of the Web.

"How would you search for him on your planet?" I ask, taking control of the mouse.

"I would ask Zook," she says, sliding the Starck vase back on her arm like it's time for less computer, more action.

"Like, you would pray?"

"No, I would kill myself. Meet Zook. Be revived by a priestess with all the answers I'd ever need."

Google feels safer.

She zips on her boots and—*zoof*—she's on her feet, ready to hunt for him old style again.

"Wait!" I call after her. "Look." I point at the screen and click on the link. "This Thursday, July sixth. At the Champs-Élysées."

She looks at the fan page I just opened. It's announcing the premiere of Johnny's new movie. She doesn't seem able to make sense of it.

"He's going to be at his new movie premiere. Here in Paris. It's in, like, six days. You know what a movie is, right?"

"Yes. A primitive form of entertainment designed to distract Earthlings from their real-life problems."

More or less. "So we know exactly where to find him on that date."

Uh-uh. She shakes her head. Not good enough. She shows me the key tattoo on her arm. It's greener and weaker than the last time

I looked at it, like it's really disappearing fast.

"I need him NOW. Today! This very second. Are you coming, or what?" She's not waiting for me anyway. She's already on her way out.

I'm about to turn off my computer and run after her. But something very familiar and unpleasant catches my eye on the screen. It's a picture of Johnny on the same fan page, and standing right behind him is . . . I click on the picture to see it full size. "Zelda! I found something!"

"What?" she barks, coming back into the room with Mom's black coat on, even though I begged her not to touch it ever again and volunteered my own old duffel coat instead.

"Malou," I say, pointing at the girl behind Johnny Depp in the picture. "I know her. It's Édouard's daughter. Sort of my stepsister. Only Mom and Édouard aren't married, so she's not *really* my stepsister."

If you search for Johnny Depp long enough on Google, you'll end up finding Malou.

Malou the pest.

Malou the black sheep.

Malou the devil.

The picture was taken in some nightclub, Malou looking joyful in the background, Johnny looking bored in the foreground. The caption reads, "Johnny and friends partying the night away."

She's just eighteen, but she's been living on her own since Édouard kicked her out of our apartment at age sixteen.

Édouard calls her "emancipated." Mom calls her "promiscuous." Mom is also known to have used stronger words to describe Malou's lifestyle.

"She writes a blog about the celebrities she knows. She's a model, too. She's been in weird movies. She's very . . . strange."

"Get her!"

"What do you mean, *get her*?"

"She knows him." Zelda taps Malou's face on the screen. "Bring her here!"

"I can't bring her here."

There are about a million rules in this apartment. One stands very high on Mom's list: Malou is never to set foot in here ever again, especially since she stole thousands of euros worth of Mom's couture and jewelry and auctioned everything at a charity gala. "It's for saving the freaking kids in Africa—chill out!" she explained when summoned to give everything back.

Zelda grabs me by my T-shirt collar and lifts me off my seat. "I've been wasting all morning on that useless piece of plastic." She points toward my iMac. "Stop challenging my orders and bring her here. NOW!"

Dad's right: Too much computer time makes people edgy.

———————

"Frog?" Malou sounds like she's eating something crunchy. "Why are you phoning me? Is Dad dead?"

Crunch crunch crunch.

"No, your dad's fine. He's having brunch with Mom."

"Oh. Are you alone in the apartment?"

"Yes." I look at Zelda. "I need you to come here."

Crunch crunch crunch.

"Why?"

"There's something I need to ask you."

"Is there champagne in the fridge?"

"I suppose," I say hesitantly.

"I'll be there in five minutes." She hangs up.

———————

73

An hour later, Zelda is turning in circles in the apartment, kicking furniture, punching walls. "Why isn't she here yet?"

I'm also turning in circles, picking up and hiding all the ridiculously expensive knickknacks that Malou might steal. "I'm not even sure she'll come at all. You can never trust anything she says. And she surrounds herself with really bad people. Like, her boyfriends always look like aging serial killers. Édouard gets a rash just from thinking about her."

Zelda shrugs. All she cares about is Johnny Depp and time running out.

Ding-dong. Here comes the hurricane.

"I'll deal with her." Zelda shoots toward the door.

I shake my head. "No way. You hide; I'll deal with her. Trust me. She sees you, and we're in trouble!"

Zelda grumbles in her dolphin talk all the way back to my closet. Malou keeps ringing. *Ding-dong. Ding-dong.* "Tadpole? Are you in there?" I hear her calling. I open the door.

"Tadpole!"

Humph! Malou hugs me and squeezes all the air out of my lungs. She always hugs me and kisses me and tells me I'm the only person she likes in this family. "I've missed you so much. Let me see you." She holds me at arm's length. "You've gotten so cute. Give you another three or four years, and you'll be, like, totally hot!"

Malou's very pretty, too, for someone so destructive. Long, jay-black hair, olive skin. As usual, she's dressed in a dozen layers of designer clothes. "Layering is very practical for shoplifting," she always explains. The result is a sort of gypsy bohemian chic look, like Esmeralda on a catwalk.

"I don't know why you haven't escaped yet," she says, zooming into the apartment.

"Because I'm fourteen."

She frowns. "So? I know people younger than you living on the streets."

Like that's supposed to inspire me.

She walks into the living room and sneers at the perfect order of things. Even the fresh layer of morning dust looks white and still.

"So cold in here. Like a tomb for the rich." She turns to me and sighs. "Poor Frog. I wish I could afford you. I'd take you with me."

And without further ado, she moves directly into Mom's room to see what couture she can snatch.

"No no no no no! You can't go in there."

"Chill out, Frog. I'm just checking what's new in the queen's closet."

She crosses Mom's room with the grace and velocity of a fashionable missile and enters the walk-in closet. She ignores the regular designer items and goes straight for the extraexpensive stuff. "Is that Saint Laurent?"

She zeroes in on the YSL piece and holds it against her. "Oh ho. *We likey*!"

"Just put the dress back, please. Look, I need something from *you* for a change."

"Something from me? Do you need drugs? I can hook you up with some really good people."

"No. No drugs."

"I get it." She gives me this sidelong look. *"Froooog!"*

"What?"

"Do you really think you're ready?"

"Ready for what?"

"Losing your virginity, silly."

Oh boy!

"It's a bit yakky, since we're practically brother and sister, but I'm honored you thought of me."

I sit down on the bed and hide my face in my hands. I don't know how she does it. She always drains the energy right out of me. "Will you just listen? It's not drugs. It's not *that*. And it's not money."

"Good. About the money. Because I was about to ask if you can lend me some. I'm totally broke!" She laughs.

"Do you know Johnny Depp?"

"Johnny?"

I nod. She drops the Saint Laurent dress on the floor and goes back to browsing through Mom's collection.

"Of course. Johnny and I are, like, totally best pals!"

She removes five or six layers of her clothes to try on one of Mom's tops.

"Do you know where I can find him? Like, where he lives?"

"Why?"

"Because."

"You tell me why, I tell you where."

"Because . . . I'm a big *fan*."

She puts on the top and pauses in front of the floor-to-ceiling mirror. "What do you think?"

"Take it off. Put it back on the rack. Tell me where to find him."

"I can get you his autograph if that's what you want. But it'll cost you."

"I need to see him in person."

She takes off her boots to try Mom's new stilettos. "Why do you need to see him?"

"I told you, I'm a big fan."

"I don't believe you. You blush when you lie."

"Please! Just tell me."

"Why?"

"Tell him immediately, Earthling! Or be ready to suffer at my hands."

Oh God! We both turn to Zelda—she's standing right there behind us in the corridor. A strong draft comes from nowhere and blows back her coat and hair. Her fists are firmly locked on her hips, and her black leather knee-high boots shine in the sunlight. She looks exactly like a Supergirl about to kick some ass.

"Man! Is that your mom's Paco Rabanne swimsuit this girl's wearing?"

9

EXPIRATION: 35 HOURS

"Where did you find her, Frog?" Malou comes out of the kitchen with a can of Mom's beluga caviar and a spoon. So much excitement has sparked her appetite.

"She's Dad's patient. Was." The way I mumble, I wonder if anyone can hear me.

"No way!" Malou's laughing. She finds us very amusing—Zelda, in her Paco Rabanne swimsuit, standing in the middle of the living room, and me beside her, blushing with all my might. "Your face was all over TV this morning," she tells Zelda. "Everyone's looking for you. And here you are with Frog, playing Spacegirl and the Little Boy." She puts a large spoonful of caviar in her mouth and frowns. "Why the Spacegirl act? Is it like a political thing? Or is it just to become famous? It's sort of brilliant, in a very dumb way."

She laughs again and sits down on the sofa. "Do you do any special tricks? Like some cool space kung fu?"

Malou demonstrates what she means by thrashing her arms around and splattering caviar all over the perfectly white sofa. I run to the kitchen to get a dishcloth. When I'm back, ready to save the sofa, Zelda isn't demonstrating any space kung fu. She's standing over Malou, staring into her eyes, her hand pressing hard on Malou's shoulder. "I will hurt you. Talk!"

"Why do you want to meet him?"

"He's my chosen one. He belongs with me."

I wish Zelda would make up something else.

"Johnny Depp and you, huh?" Malou drops the spoon in the caviar and the caviar pot on the coffee table. She looks up at Zelda and pushes her hand off her shoulder. "I'm sorry, darling, I don't think you're his type."

"GET HER OFF ME!"

It's that Vahalalian short temper again. Zelda's sitting on top of Malou on the floor, but instead of singing her a cute intergalactic lullaby, she's holding her down by the throat.

I don't blame her. Malou can really get on your nerves.

"Tell. Me. Where. To. Find. Him!" Zelda says, banging Malou's head on the carpet: *Bang. Bang. Bang. Bang.*

"Da. Vid. Help. Me!"

Forget about Zelda forbidding me to ever touch her again. I grab her by the shoulders and pull as hard as I can. "Zelda! Stop! She's practically my sister!"

She stops strangling Malou to push me away. "Don't interfere, Pudin. This is standard Vahalalian interrogation protocol."

"THIS GIRL IS NUTS!" Malou screams, once she can breathe again. "Tell her to get off me!"

Malou searches for something in the pocket of the top layer of her many skirts. A knife? A gun? A picture of an ex-boyfriend?

Pepper spray! She points it at Zelda's face. "Slap me one more time, and I'll—"

Zelda slaps her hard across the face. Which is another lesson learned: Never challenge a Vahalalian.

Malou closes her eyes and triggers the spray. Nothing happens. It's empty.

"Shit! Asshole!" Malou shakes it, trying to squeeze out a last drop. "The guy I stole it from said it was full. You can't trust anyone!"

Zelda snatches the spray and throws it to me. She grabs Malou's hands. "I will crush every single bone in these hands unless you tell me where to find my chosen one."

"You can torture me all you want, bikini girl. I will never give the address, phone number, or any embarrassing physical details of any of my celebrity friends. Not for all the money in the world."

"What about nine hundred fifty-two euros?" I ask, squatting beside her.

She turns to me. "What did you just say, Tadpole?"

"It's all my savings—nine hundred fifty-two euros. All yours if you tell us where to find him."

"Deal!"

———

"What am I buying exactly?" I ask.

We're sitting in my bedroom, negotiating around bottles of diet ginger ale.

"For this kind of money, I'll deliver him to you. Packed, cleaned, and ready to go. You can do whatever you want with him." She's about to drink some ginger ale. She stops, looking at me sideways again, like she's having second thoughts. "By the way, what are you going to do with him? You're not going to *harm* him, are you?"

"No, nobody's going to get hurt. Right?"

Zelda shrugs, like, *I don't know yet.* "I don't trust her, dwarf."

"Dwarf?" Malou laughs her head off. "And you give me shit for calling you Frog."

Sigh.

"Do we have a deal, then?" I ask.

"Nope. No money, no deal."

"It's in the bank, in my savings account." I was saving it to buy the ultracool Vespa scooter that was supposed to make me popular. "I can't get it before Monday."

"So Monday is the day you get to meet Johnny."

"I cannot wait that long," Zelda says, pushing her ginger ale bottle out of the way. "I will torture her instead."

"All right, all right, all right! *Chill out!*" Malou hides her hands behind her back to avoid additional torturing. "I trust you, Tadpole. I give you Johnny over the weekend. You give me the money on Monday. Jesus! Someone give this girl a Xanax."

––––––––

Malou has a car. It must have been nice looking not so long ago, sporty and all that. Expensive. Red. Now it's smashed up like someone chewed it with a mouthful of mud and spat it out in this parking place on a street right behind the Pantheon.

"My ex-boyfriend gave me this piece of trash. It used to be his wife's car. He's divorcing her now. They have issues."

I'll say.

"Hop in the backseat, Tadpole."

I knew she would say that. It's a small coupe with no real backseat.

The inside of the car reminds me of the inside of her apartment. She pushes down magazines, fast-food trash, empty plastic bottles, old dirty clothes, and a couple pairs of shoes to make room for Zelda in the passenger seat.

Surprisingly, the car stinks of cigarettes.

"You're smoking now?"

She used to say, "If smoking is so cool, how come Dad's doing it?"

"My ex-boyfriend's wife did. I could never get rid of the stench."

Malou's speeding down the riverbank highway. She's driving us to a bar near the Champs-Élysées. According to Malou, Johnny Depp owns the place. It's not like he's going to be there mixing drinks, but she knows a waiter who knows someone who knows everyone.

"I love the black-coat-and-swimsuit fashion statement," Malou says, glancing at Zelda. "And the broken vase on your arm—very fashion forward. Did you know it's a Starck? It's worth gazillions."

I wish she was able to talk and watch the road at the same time.

"Imagine the Queen Bee's face if she saw Spacegirl in her *beloved* black coat. She'd probably die of a stroke before she could even start yelling at you. Think of it, the old bitch dying. You'd finally be free, Tadpole."

"Don't talk about Mom like that." I hate it when Malou or anyone talks about Mom. I know she's a dragon with a taste for blood, but she loves me. At least a few hours per week. Mostly on Sundays.

"He's funny, this little guy," Malou tells Zelda. "She's such a bitch to him, but he never bites back. I don't know, Frog, you must be bottling it up."

I wish 952 euros could also buy her silence.

"Do you have parents, Spacegirl?"

"They have been destroyed."

No wonder she comes across as a bit cold.

"I don't mean in your space fantasy life. I mean in real life."

"Her parents are dead, okay?" I say so Malou will stop asking questions, but that's not knowing Malou.

"Yeah? How did they die?"

"My mother was decapitated during the Unholy Wars. My father was disintegrated as he tried to escape the Tower of Tor. He was a violent and undisciplined specimen from the planet Bova."

Ha. Now I know where she gets that temper from.

"I wish my father was disintegrated, too," Malou says thoughtfully. "Just imagine. Beamed. *Zouf.* Gone. A heap of ashes with his stupid Armani glasses on top. Wouldn't that be cool, huh? Tadpole? Can you pass me that bag of chips you're sitting on?"

Malou disappears into the bar, leaving me and Zelda to wait in the car.

"Zelda?" I pick up the bag of chips Malou was munching on.

"Yes?" She turns to me, and I offer her the chips. Another Earthling invention worth discovering.

"You know, it might not be a good idea to tell everyone who you are and where you come from."

She takes a potato chip and smells it suspiciously. "They ask. I answer."

"But if you tell people something else, they might just let you be and not try to lock you up in a nuthouse."

"Something else?" She bites off a small corner of the chip and chews it slowly, like she's conducting one of her experiments in gustative biochemistry. She seems satisfied with the results and throws the rest of it into her mouth.

"Like, you don't need to tell everyone you're from another planet and that your father was turned into ashes with a laser beam."

"But I *am* from another planet, and my father *was* disintegrated, though there was no laser beam. It was an antimatter field."

Sigh.

"Make up a story. Be creative."

"Creative?" She shrugs, reaching for more chips.

"Don't you have movies, fairy tales, books on Vahalal?"

"Yes, we have books, of course, but reading or producing what you Earthlings call fairy tales is a sin. We stick to science, war strategy, and Zookology." She takes the whole bag from me. So far, she's very happy with Earthling junk food.

"So you never lie?"

"No." Chips.

"Have you ever tried?"

"I told you. It is a sin." Chips.

"Could you say . . . um . . . 'My name is Maria, and I come from . . . Sweden'?"

She stops chewing. "Why would I say that?"

"I don't know. Just give it a try, okay?"

"My-name-is-Maria-and-I-come-from-Sweden."

No. It sounded totally wrong.

"Maybe you should put more heart into it. Like, if I asked you, How old are you, *Maria*?"

"I am three hundred twenty-five years old. That is, three hundred twenty-five on Vahalal, the planet I come from." Chips.

"Forget it."

"That was nine hundred fifty-two euros easily earned."

Malou's all happy with herself as she gets back into the car. She winks at me. "Johnny will be at a party in Le Marais tonight. An art gallery opening or something. And now I'm invited by this totally reliable guy and I'll be bringing you, Spacegirl. I can say you're my new girlfriend or something."

"Wait a minute. What about me?" I ask.

"What about you, Tadpole?"

"You're getting me in, too, aren't you?"

"Sorry. It's not a kids' party. No sponge cake. No clown. No balloons. And no *you*."

Ha! "Zelda, tell her!"

"Tell me what?" Malou asks.

"That you *need* me!"

Malou gives her a look, like, "I'm sorry, Zelda. They're cute, but they're very naive at his age."

"I don't believe this!" I say.

"Believe it. I'll drive you home. Zelda's coming to my place. I'll find her something less Lady Gaga to wear. She meets Johnny Depp tonight. We meet in front of your bank on Monday. Ciao, Tadpole."

10
EXPIRATION: 33 HOURS

We're living in a cruel world. No, let me rephrase that. We're living in a cruel universe.

"This is not a good plan. I have a bad feeling about it," I say, refusing to get out of the car.

"Out!" Malou shouts, throwing a handful of chips at me.

I extricate myself hesitantly, brushing away crumbs. We're double-parked right in front of my building. I have this feeling that Zelda could never survive without me. Or I could never survive without Zelda. I'm not sure which anymore. Whatever it is, I refuse to close the door on her, and I want to throw myself on my knees right here on the pavement, grab her, and beg her to take me with them.

"What about the Pudin thing? You said we were supposed to be like *this*." I knot my hands together to show how tight we're supposed to be. "Aren't we, like, breaking one of those really important Vahalalian rules that can't be broken or else the universe melts?"

She nods like she gets my point and turns to Malou. "Are you absolutely sure I cannot take my Pudin along?"

"No, you cannot take your pudding to this kind of party. They won't let him in." Malou leans over Zelda to take hold of the door handle. "It's your choice. Him"—she nods toward me—"or Johnny boy."

Zelda shakes her head. "You've been a very good Pudin. I will never forget you, Earthling."

Slam! Malou closes the door, and the universe melts. "Love you, Tadpole!" she screams gaily through the open window. "See you on Monday. Have that cash ready for me. Thanks for flying Air Malou, and have a lovely day!" She laughs and drives away.

The car veers off at the crossroad. Zelda waves hesitantly. I want to wave back, but it's too late. She's gone for good. So fast. *Poof.* Vanished from my life.

I enter my building and decide to climb the stairs. I can't stand the idea of finding myself locked inside the elevator.

My heart is broken. David Gershwin, killed by a Vahalalian. Zelda. For Chrissake! I close my eyes. Even thinking her name is painful.

Who's going to sing to me now?

I reach our floor. I don't want to go in. Malou's right. It's so cold inside this apartment, and I don't mean the temperature. It's cold. And small. And empty. And I'm trapped in there for years and years to come, breathing their cigarette smoke and listening to them yelling at each other until their voices break.

I unlock the door and walk in.

"David."

"Dad!"

He's standing in the corridor, a cup of coffee in his hand. Past him, I see Mom sitting on the sofa. She's uncharacteristically quiet.

Two of the uniformed policemen assigned to bring Zelda back to Cornouaille stand up silently. I don't like the way they're staring at me. Like they've all been waiting for me.

"Where is she, David?" Dad asks.

"I . . ."

"David? Did you . . . ?" Mom's voice is shaking, like something really horrible has happened. "Did you really give this crazy girl my black coat?"

———————

I hear them calling my name and running after me in the staircase.

I didn't wait. I didn't explain. I didn't say "Hello" or "I'm sorry for the coat," or "Don't kill me, Mother." I followed my instincts and ran, ran, ran, as if my life depended on it.

I rush out of the building and choose not to go through the park. I turn at the Théâtre de l'Odéon. I'm not much of a runner (it's a size thing), but hell, I know each corner of each street of this labyrinth known as the Quartier Latin. One right: rue de Condé. One left: rue Saint-Sulpice. One right: rue des Canettes. One left. And down the subway ramp at Saint-Sulpice station. I jump over the turnstile and catch a train right before the doors close.

Look at me! I'm a gangster, a hustler, the master of FREAKING lobsters. I AM THE MAN!

Phew.

Wait a second . . .

I'm totally cooked.

———————

"*Velkome to zee Penthouse*," Malou says, opening the door of her studio-apartment-revolting-little-cupboard-of-a-place. She's not even surprised to see me. "We thought you'd come here."

"How did you know?"

"You should watch more TV, Frog. Considering."

Her place is exactly the way I remembered, like a miniaturized dump site. She has no furniture. Everything lies directly on the floor—trash, clothes, magazines, the mattress Zelda's sitting on.

"Here. Come. Have a seat beside your girlfriend." Malou pushes me down on the mattress. Zelda is hugging her knees tight against her chest, completely avoiding looking at me.

"Hello," I say hesitantly.

"You're making my mission IMPOSSIBLE!" she barks back.

"I . . ." I shake my head in disbelief. I've done absolutely nothing wrong. I point toward the door. "For your information, I just escaped from the police. They were running after me. A whole bunch of them. And I was, like . . ." I show them with my hand: *zoom zing boom!* "I wish you could have seen me—I was WILD!"

"Wild's the word, huh, Zeldie?" Malou teases Zelda with a good push on her shoulder. "Let me show you something that might be of interest." She sits between us and opens her laptop. "It's all over the place. It's like you're this total YouTube sensation."

She clicks the YouTube video to full screen. "Ta-da."

I recognize the Notre Dame bridge. It's a stupid cell phone video. The picture pans from the cathedral to . . . Zelda. Then to me. Zelda leans over me. And . . . OMIGOD!

She's FRENCH KISSING me! And there are already 199,995 views and 52 comments!

Damn you, YouTube!

"Aaaaah, love. I feel all gooey just sitting between you guys." Malou laughs.

"This has nothing to do with the concept of love." Zelda sinks deeper behind her knees. "Love is a sin. I was sampling his DNA. It was an experiment in gustative biochemistry."

"Yeah, I'd say you were sampling him real bad, sister. Look at that tongue going! It's like you're trying to eat him."

The kiss just won't stop. I didn't remember that she'd had her hands in my hair and held me so tight. It doesn't look like an "experiment in gustative biochemistry" at all. It looks like two lovers passionately making out over the Seine. And my heart is going to explode if someone doesn't stop that video soon.

It finally freezes at the point where Zelda's lips part from mine. My eyes are shut. I look lost. She stares at me, smiling, looking truly happy. How could I have missed that back there on the bridge?

The screen goes black.

"Replay?" Malou asks. She laughs again.

———

Malou's going out to borrow some props from a friend, like a wig and a new coat that could fit Zelda's long frame. "I'm sure you two need some privacy, anyway," Malou says, winking at me again. "Feel free to *sample* more. This apartment is an emancipated zone."

She turns back just before leaving her studio. "You know, that smooch on the bridge explains a lot. She was all cranky after we dumped you."

———

We're alone again. We haven't moved an inch since we watched the video.

"I think we should abort tonight's outing and work on a new strategy," I say hesitantly.

Silence.

Silence.

And then suddenly, Zelda periscopes up from behind her knees. "I wasn't cranky at all. This Malou creature is a very unreliable specimen. Travelers dispose of their Pudins frequently. You mean absolutely nothing to me."

She periscopes back down while a ball of pain grows like an acid sponge in my stomach.

Silence.

Silence.

More freaking silence.

It's my turn to be cranky. "What's wrong with you, Zelda?!" I'm just one tiny notch short of yelling.

"Nothing is wrong with me."

"Don't you ever feel *anything*?"

She looks at me blankly. "No, I do not."

"I don't believe you." Someone who doesn't feel anything doesn't smile the way she did after we kissed.

"Fine," she confesses. "I feel rage sometimes—I want to beat up and kill things. But that is a sin, too."

She means feeling rage is a sin. Beating up and killing things is absolutely fine.

"And besides rage?"

She frowns. "Besides rage, what?"

"Any other emotions?"

"Of course not. Emotions are poison."

"When we kissed"—I point toward Malou's laptop—"you looked like . . . you were feeling a . . . like, serious bunch of emotions. You did!" And 199,995 YouTube viewers are my witnesses.

"No, I didn't! I . . ."

"You *what*?"

"I don't like this conversation at all," she says coldly and—
SLAM!

The conversation is over anyway, since Malou bursts back into her studio and goes, "Omigod! We're totally in trouble." She rushes to the only window to check the street below. "I'm being *followed*!"

EXPIRATION: 31 HOURS

Malou is right. By the time we stumble out of her studio, we can hear people running up the seven floors.

Zelda looks up to the skylight and decides in a flash. "To the roof!"

Malou: "No, there's nothing on the roof!"

Me: "Think about what Mom's going to do to us!"

Malou (after a short pause): "To the roof!"

Zelda is already climbing the ladder. She glances back at us. "Faster, Earthlings!"

I climb up the ladder second, Malou behind me. I pop my head outside. Malou's absolutely right. There's nothing up here—just a collection of slopes leading to certain death. But there's no stopping Zelda. She's already gliding toward the next building.

———————

Malou and I walk carefully step by step, hugging each other and cursing profusely. Zelda is doing the gazelle thing again, hopping and flying from one roof to the next as if she has wings, calling back to us and complaining about the unbearable slowness of all Earthlings.

"Hey! Kids! Stop!"

We turn back. The bald policeman from Cornouaille pops his head through the skylight. "You're going to kill yourselves!"

I couldn't agree more.

Step, step. Oops. Step, step. Sliiiide. Omigod!

"How did they find us? Did you tell them Zelda was with me?" Malou asks.

"No, I didn't tell them *anything*."

Step, step. Oops.

"Do you have a cell phone? Something they could track?"

"No. No cell phone." I gave up my cell phone ages ago. No one ever called, which just reminded me how unpopular I am.

Sliiiiide.

"Stop talking," I beg her. "You're going to kill us."

"Kids! Come back," the bald man calls after us as he climbs onto the roof. "We're here to help you."

"Where did you phone me from this morning?"

"From home."

"Frog! What were you thinking?"

Step, ste . . . sliiiide. Aaaah!

I grab Malou's sleeve right before she falls ten floors down. When she's done screaming, she offers this piece of advice: "Next time you're hiding a fugitive in your bedroom closet, use a pay phone!"

———

The good news: We're still alive.

The bad news: Malou looks like she just swallowed a live bug, and we're trapped.

"I can't do it!" she shouts.

I understand. It's a killer. It's a gap between two buildings. Zelda jumped over it like it was nothing; I *just* made it and nearly fell. Malou's still on the other side, refusing to move, even though the bald man chasing us is closing the distance fast. I don't blame Malou. When you look down, all you can see is a guaranteed splash headfirst onto the cobblestones of a tiny, dark courtyard.

"Think of the money!" I shout. "Jump!"

"Keep your money! Leave me alone!"

"I will get her," Zelda says, getting ready for another gazelle hop.

Too late for that. Malou's cooked. The bald man slides down the last tiny piece of roof behind her and grabs her by the top layer of her clothes.

"Don't you move, now," he says, his voice shaking.

Zelda sighs. "Damn Earthlings." Then she . . . she . . . *what*?

She disappeared from my side. I mean . . . she was there. And then—*POOF*, MAGIC!—she's gone. Then—*POW!*—she reappears beside Malou and the guy.

"You must be kidding me," the man says, right before she smashes the broken Starck vase in his face. He drops onto the roof like a wet mop.

Malou wanted space kung fu, and space kung fu she got. And now she's screaming bloody murder as Zelda grabs her around the waist and forces her to jump over the gap with her.

They land at my feet and Malou collapses like a package of soft spaghetti. I squat in front of her. "Are you . . . ?" I shrug. I'm sort of at a loss for words since Zelda did her magic trick.

"Your girlfriend"—Malou nods toward Zelda—"she's not normal."

"Was that . . . ?" I forget what she called that thing.

"Space Splash!" Zelda confirms proudly. "I am no longer Space Flopped." She's nearly smiling, like, *Come on, Earthlings, bring it on now!*

———————

We're hiding inside a pirate's boat on a small playground near Canal Saint-Martin, a few blocks from Malou's place. She hasn't completely recovered yet. She's eyeing Zelda sideways, waiting for something else weird to happen, like an alien bursting out of her chest or something.

"Did you kill him?"

"I don't think so."

"You disappeared," Malou whispers. "Like, you can be invisible and stuff."

"It's called Space Splashing," I explain, like I'm a freaking Vahalalian expert now.

Malou slaps her forehead. "Omigod! She's really from outer space, isn't she, Frog?"

I shrug. Apparently so.

"This is sooo totally great. A real Spacegirl! Get out of here!" She opens her arms and gives Zelda a big, friendly hug. "I've always dreamed that something like this would happen to me."

Zelda pushes her away. "Physical contact is not required by protocol, Earthling."

"Ha. Listen to her talk ET. 'Physical contact is not required by protocol.' I love it." Suddenly, Malou loses some of that smile. "Wait a second, guys. Why would an extraterrestrial want to meet someone like Johnny Depp?"

"Zelda, please," I beg, "you do not need to explain this to her."

"A planet of girls!" Malou screams after Zelda's done explaining absolutely everything about her mission. "I'd be totally into that."

"Can you be quieter?" I ask, since we're now walking down the street, completely exposed, on our way to retrieve Malou's car before any good citizens spot us.

"I love the Tower of Tor thingy. I'd love to lock up some of my ex-boyfriends. The scumbags!"

She fishes her car keys out of her back pocket.

"No more men, no more trouble, huh? It's so totally obvious! You girls up there have it all figured out." She nods toward the street corner. "I'm parked just around here."

Dead right. The second we turn the corner, we see her smashed-up car and four uniformed policemen inspecting it. One of them immediately points at us.

"I think this is our cue to RUN!" I shout, and—*zooof*—we take off.

Malou takes the lead. Not a great idea, if you ask me. "This way. No, that way. No! Sorry, this other way. Oh God. Faster, Frog!" One thing everyone should know about Malou: She runs away from the police like she lives—going in all directions at the same time and never choosing one path and sticking to it.

She stops suddenly. "Sorry, guys, I—"

"She screwed up again!" I yell.

Zelda slaps the wall right in front of us. Malou has led us straight into a dead end. We're so busted; the cops behind us even slow down to catch their breath.

"We're going to do this nice 'n' easy," one of them shouts from the other side of the street. He holds his rib cage. I guess running isn't his thing, either.

"Can you do some more of your space kung fu?" Malou demonstrates by doing some random arm and leg movements. She adds sound effects: "Kai! Kai! Kai!"

"I sure will," Zelda says, taking a combat stance and getting ready to Space Splash them to hell.

"Hey! I said nice 'n' easy," the cop repeats. "No kung-fu shit."

Bing bang boom!

The policemen turn around.

"What the f—," one of them starts.

It's not Zelda. She's still beside me. But three girls have just appeared right behind the policemen—like, freaking *poof*! They're very much like Zelda, same age, same size, and same mean expression that says "I'm going to get you, you male scum." Otherwise, they have many more facial tattoos, piercings, and dreadlocks for hair. And their choice of outfit is like worn-out paramilitary clothing, put together in an urban-squadron-from-hell fashion.

Before the policemen can understand the nightmare they're in for, the girls draw batons and—*chaching badabing boom*—the four men are lying on the ground, moaning.

"Are those your friends?" I ask carefully.

They don't even put away their batons as they approach us.

"Somehow I preferred the cops," Malou says, backing up all the way to the wall.

One of the girls pushes up her sleeve and shows the inside of her arm as she approaches. She has the exact same tattoo as Zelda, the one saying she's a Vahalalian, only it's been covered by a completely new tattoo—a green snake, the same snake that was on that letter Dad received.

"Valk exiles," Zelda says grimly.

I want to ask Zelda what they want from us, but they don't give me the chance. The three girls start singing a weird whale song, and I immediately feel terribly sleepy.

I bet they're doctors, too.

EXPIRATION: 21 HOURS

The first thing I see when I open my eyes is Malou and Zelda looking down at me. And then just Zelda slapping me across the face.

"Oooouch! Aren't we on the same team?!"

"Keep those eyes open!" Malou lifts me off the floor and shakes me hard. "Come on! Wakey, wakey!"

"Ask him his name," Zelda says, getting ready for another good whack.

"What's your name, Frog?"

"I wish you'd stop calling me that."

"He's fine," Malou says, dropping me back on the floor.

"Where are we?" I sit up and look around. We're in a small room with no windows. An old projector is lying on the floor, and the wall in front of me is covered with large maps of Europe. Zelda and Malou are sitting against the wall beside me.

"We don't know. It's like a cell."

I stand up groggily. "And the good news is?"

Zelda shrugs. "There is no good news, Pudin. Exiles are Vahala-lian outcasts. Failures. War criminals. Mass murderers."

"Great! I love meeting new people." My legs feel soft like marsh-mallow. I lean against a map of Europe. "By the way, what do they want with us, besides murder?"

"Quiz us on geography?" Malou suggests.

"Hope so. I'm an ace at geography." Thanks to my addiction to atlases and hours of planning imaginary travels around the globe.

"I don't know what they want." Zelda stands up, readjusting the Starck vase on her arm. "We will soon find out."

She's right. Someone is unlocking the door. And—*zaam!*—we're standing in front of three angry-looking girls.

"Whatever happens, don't look them in the eye," Zelda says. "Looking a Valk in the eye is a deadly sin."

One of the girls says something, and whatever it is, it's not French. It sounds like the dolphin talk Zelda used to make me her Pudin. *Squikitikiki.*

"They are taking us to the mother," Zelda translates.

"Who's the mother?" Malou and I ask at the same time, hiding behind Zelda and doing our best not to look those girls in the eye.

"Their leader, the eldest exile."

A grandma in dreads!

The girls push us out of the cell and escort us down a long cor-ridor. It's dark and damp and dirty. There are windows, but they've been painted over or covered by newspapers.

Here is a thing about Vahalalian exiles: They hate daylight and cleaning up things.

"This is a school," Malou says as we walk past rows of coat hangers and pass in front of classrooms piled high with trash.

"Look." Malou points at a group of girls ahead in the corridor, about a dozen of them, with different tattoos, piercings, and weird haircuts and identical hateful looks on their faces.

"No, don't look at them," Zelda says as we walk toward them. "See the markings on their faces?"

Yes, I can see them now. Their faces are covered in dark green tribal tattoos, just like the three girls escorting us. It looks cool, in a terrifying sort of way.

"Only Valks register their killings on their faces. Keep walking and look away, Pudin."

I try to keep looking away while walking toward their group. Not an easy thing, since:

1. They're painfully beautiful.

2. They're fighting and Space Splashing like it's nothing. *Poof*, disappear, *poof*, reappear, jab, jab, cross, baton, and kick, *poof*, redisappear.

"I'm never going to get used to this Space-Splashy-thingy," Malou says.

"And you won't have to if you keep looking at them, Earthlings. They will include you in their practice routine and destroy you."

I look at my sneakers as we pass by. Being destroyed by a dozen gorgeous girls armed with batons only sounds good on paper.

"Are they all looking for their chosen ones, like you?"

"Valks remain virgin and childless. They focus on fighting, killing, and praying to Zook."

I guess it takes all kinds.

"Why are they here?" I ask.

"They've been punished and exiled. Most of them for murders that were not directly dictated by Zook. War crimes. Unjustified massacres. I SAID DON'T LOOK AT THEM, PUDIN!"

"Oops. Sorry!" Couldn't resist glancing back.

Zelda pushes me forward.

"Why do they all look so angry?" I ask. It's like someone just stomped on their combat boots or confiscated their favorite weapons.

"They've been away from Vahalal for too long."

"How long is long?"

"Hundreds of years for some. Thousands for others."

Wait a second. "A thousand years?!"

"We live much longer than you Earthlings."

"But . . . they all look about the same age." Just like Zelda, about sixteen.

"We perfected our DNA. We do not age. We can potentially live forever."

That *is* long.

"Those are Travelers, like me," Zelda says, pointing at another group of girls farther down the corridor. "It is okay to look at them."

"What's wrong with them?" Malou asks. "They're like—"

"Insane," confirms Zelda.

They're dressed in old rags, pieces of clothing and material randomly tied around their bodies, like sexy young hoboes. Some of them rock back and forth, lunatic style. Others walk on all fours, picking up bits of crap from the floor and throwing them into their mouths, performing gustative biochemistry on dust balls like mad scientists.

"When a Traveler fails to find her chosen one, she loses all purpose in life," Zelda says. "She ends up like her." She nods toward a Vahalalian hobo who has just found an old piece of gum. She throws it in her mouth and chews it enthusiastically. No wonder Zelda is so eager to find Johnny Depp.

———

The Valks drag us into a school gym packed with about a hundred more girls like them. They stare at us with enough intensity to set my hair on fire.

They make us sit on three exercise balls in front of another angry teenager. "Don't look her in the eye," Zelda says. "This is the mother, and she's a Valk."

I knew that! There's not an inch of her face that's not covered with the green tribal markings. And holy Armani! She's really into strong fashion statements, too: She wears a black vinyl outfit with a long black cape. Snake tattoos twist around her neck, wrists, and ankles and all around her face, framing the markings that sum up a lifetime of murders. Her gray blue eyes are so intense I don't need Zelda to tell me not to look into them for too long. She stands exactly in the middle of the basketball court, where you'd expect to find your PE teacher, only I'm pretty sure she's not about to tell us to drop and give her twenty. She speaks, and it's immediately obvious this isn't going to be a French class, either.

Zelda answers with the very same sort of tongue-clicking dolphin gibberish: *Quikidizikzik quikidizokzok.*

"Are we in trouble?" I ask when they're done squeaking.

"Yes. We're in trouble."

Good, that's one thing clarified. "What do they want?"

"They want what every Vahalalian desires most."

"We want to return to Vahalal," the mother says with a dry, dusty, creaking, mummy-type voice. "And Zelda will give us the key."

"Mother," Zelda says, falling to her knees to address her, "Zook forbids us to open the door or return without our chosen one."

"CHOSEN ONES DON'T EXIST!" the mother shouts, as if Zelda hit her in the gut. "Three thousand years I've been on this planet! I've seen hundreds of Travelers come here and fail. So we Valks say chosen ones are nothing but a myth. Travelers are wrong. All men are RATS!"

"Scumbags!"

"Liars!"

"Cowards!"

"Pigs!"

The girls in that gym have a pretty definite opinion of male Earthlings.

"We Valk exiles," the mother declares, "challenge the Book of Zook and the obsolete beliefs of Travelers and declare there is no good man on this testosterone-infested planet." There: heretic and proud of it. "Don't force us to torture or kill you or the two Earthlings. Just transfer the key to me while it's still valid, and let us go home."

What did she just say?

TORTURE?! KILL?!

"Frog!" Malou shouts. "Nine hundred fifty-two euros is, like, way underpaid!"

"You are the one who is wrong!" Zelda shoots to her feet as if she's done with diplomacy. "The Book of Zook warns us that finding our chosen one is an almost impossible task. Zook tells us of the doubts and failures. But Zook also tells us that being a Vahalalian is to keep fighting and searching. So you can torture me. You can kill these Earthlings. It won't change a thing. I won't disobey our laws and pass you the key, for I have already found my chosen one."

Ooooh, aaaah! *A chosen one! A chosen one!* It sends a shock wave through the school gym. Even the failed Travelers stop chewing on dust balls to listen to what Zelda has to say.

"Did you sample him?" the mother asks.

"Not yet."

They all shake their heads. False alarm! No sampling, no deal.

"I will sample him soon. His name is Johnny Depp."

"THE ACTOR?"

"Yes, the actor." And the crowd goes wild, like no matter what planet you're from, if you're a girl, Johnny's big news.

"SILENCE!" orders the mother. She sits down on her exercise ball once the initial Johnny Depp shock has passed. "So be it, Traveler," she says softly. "Tena! Lena! Pela!"

The three girls who reduced the cops to mumbling goo rise up from the assembly and step forward. "Get me Brad Pitt. Lock him in a safe location. Wait for my instructions. We will exchange him against Zelda's goodwill."

"She said Johnny Depp, your highness."

"Brad Pitt, Johnny Depp, Robert freaking Pattinson! I don't care. We will abduct every single Hollywood stud if it will bring us back to Vahalal. GET HIM!"

And off they go with lethal looks on their faces and batons under their belts. I tell you, if I were Johnny, I'd start running in the other direction.

"What are you going to do to him?" Zelda cries in anger.

"Nothing, if you give me the key. But if you don't . . ." She slaps the palm of her hand with a closed fist, like . . . *squash*! Good-bye, Johnny. "No more chosen one for you, my girl."

"You cannot do that! It is heresy! Valks are supposed to help Travelers in their holy quest."

"Believe me, Zelda. After you have spent more than a hundred years on this pathetic little planet, you'll eat your own tongue just for a chance to get away."

———————

The mother waves her hand, talks dolphin, and Malou and Zelda are led from the room. "Bring me the boy," she says, and a Valk pushes me toward her.

"Interesting," she breathes, grabbing my face and squeezing. The snakes on her wrist look like they could bite. "Zelda must find you fascinating."

Ha! "Trust me, I'm the last thing to fascinate Zelda in the entire universe."

Ouch! She squeezes harder. I get it: *Do not* contradict a Valk either. "The first young male she sees. And you're cute like a box of ducklings." She turns my face east and west, then pulls me toward her by the neck. Now it's the snakes around her face that seem to want a piece of me. "So young, so innocent," she purrs in my ear. "Pity you all turn into pigs as you get older." And with that, she pushes me back into the hands of her disciples.

"Zelda is not used to emotions," the mother calls after me as they drag me back to our cell. "I envy her. Nothing's more beautiful than a first feeling."

13

EXPIRATION: 18 HOURS

"She's making me dizzy going in circles like that," Malou complains. "Tell her to stop."

There's no point talking to Zelda right now. Her answer to everything is no, no, no!

No, I won't stop walking in circles and kicking and punching the agricultural maps of Europe. No, I won't disobey Zookian laws. No, I won't give them the key.

She checks her forearm. "I don't have time for this!"

"How would you pass this thing to them?" Malou asks.

"I can transfer it to any of them during sexual intercourse."

Malou puts her hands over my ears. "Zeldie! You're going to permanently traumatize the poor kid! You Spacegirls are so totally D-I-R-T-Y!" she shrieks.

I push her hands away. "Don't worry. I've seen and heard enough during the last twenty-four hours to spend the rest of my life in therapy."

"It doesn't matter how I would give it to them," Zelda says finally, stopping her pacing and sitting down in a corner of our cell. She strokes the key, like she's trying to give it a little extra life. "Giving them the key would mean failing. Didn't you see what happens to a failed Traveler?"

True. I can't imagine someone like Zelda dressing in rags and eating dust balls for the next few centuries.

"What about us?" Malou asks. "The mother girl mentioned torture and FREAKING MURDER."

"Is there a Zookian law against letting two innocent Earthlings get tortured or killed?" I ask hopefully.

Zelda thinks about it for a nanosecond and then shakes her head. "No. Zook does not care about the lives of Earthlings."

———————

I can't stop thinking about what the mother said. Fascinating? Me? *No way!*

I catch Zelda's eye.

"What?" she barks.

"Nothing," I say, pretending to study a map of the European Union as it was in 1989. I'm studying Austria when there's a loud thump on the door.

"What was that?"

Zelda puts a finger over my lips before I can say another word.

I'm not dreaming—something's definitely happening outside. Malou's already beside the door, listening. "It sounds like they're fighting out there." She jumps back.

There was a blunt noise, like a sack of potatoes hitting the floor. Then someone unlocks the door, and a group of Valks come in.

They squeak a bit. Zelda squeaks back, and then they do something quite unexpected: They kneel *right* in front of us like Zelda did in front of the mother.

"Ahem, excuse us, *Zeldie*." Malou clears her throat. "We wouldn't mind getting a bit of *that* decoded."

"They're going to disobey the mother and let us go."

"Why?"

"They still believe in their duty to help a Traveler. They have faith in my holy quest for a chosen one."

"You guys should totally rebel," Malou tells the Valks. "I mean, your old queen is so totally overdoing the *mother* thing. You know, I had a teacher just like her. The old bag!"

We (collectively): *"Shhhh!"*

"The mother is a good leader," one of the Valks says as we cross a ruined playground in front of the abandoned school. "She lost faith in Travelers a few centuries ago, just like the rest of us."

"When Zelda talked tonight," says another one, "she reminded us of what we had forgotten long ago: what it means to be Vahalalian."

We climb over a fence and land in a parking lot. I turn back. A poster says that the school is due to be demolished soon. There's also graffiti over the poster. The Vahalalian snake tag: Beware! Keep out!

"How long have you been living here?" I ask.

"We moved in just a year ago. Finding a place for the Sanctuary is becoming harder, and our group keeps expanding."

It's a curse: more and more Spacegirls, less and less good real estate to snatch.

"Why don't you integrate into our society? Go to school. Find jobs. Rent apartments. Live like us."

"We want nothing to do with your society. We detest Earthlings. We loathe your primitive civilization."

There. Now I know.

They escort us to the local train station. I know exactly where we are. We're right beside the Stade de France. The ultramodern soccer stadium looks like a gigantic UFO. It's something past midnight, and we need to get to Johnny before the three girls after him show him some of that baton boogie.

There are a few young people waiting on the platform for the next night train to arrive. They don't pay attention to us. They're lost in their own thoughts, and I wonder how many of them know what I know. Could there be anyone else from outer space on this platform? Who's an Earthling, and who's *something else*?

A few days ago, my life was flat, dull, and boring. Everyone looked the same. People were just people, like pieces of paper. Now that I've met Zelda, every person has become interesting. Imagine: They might be hiding a deep, meaningful secret, like an intergalactic past or an extraordinary quest.

One of the Valks gives Zelda a piece of paper. "That's his address."

Malou snatches the paper and reads it. "How did you get Johnny's personal address?"

"We asked Zook, but she refused to intervene. So we visited the hot night spots and found a man who would sell the information. We tortured him."

Valks are so efficient! I read the address over Malou's shoulder. It's written with real shaky handwriting. I bet the poor guy who wrote it didn't get 952 euros.

"Good luck," one of the Valks says as our train comes into the station.

We get in. "Girl power!" Malou shouts. She gives them the *V* for victory sign as the train doors close. One of the girls returns the *V* hesitantly, and they Space Splash away into the dark.

"They totally dig me," Malou says, sitting down with us as the train departs. "But I've always been a girl magnet. Right, Zelda?" She taps Zelda's knee.

"Touch me again and die, Earthling."

"Sometimes the chemistry's just not there." Malou removes her hand, stands up, and walks around the train car trying to bum a cigarette from one of the other passengers.

14

EXPIRATION: 17 HOURS

"It's one of these streets," Malou says, glancing around for more clues.

We're lost, walking down Quai d'Anjou on Île Saint-Louis, right along the Seine, because Malou said she knew *exactly* where to find the address on that piece of paper.

"You have no idea where you're going, do you?" I say. "You were just bullshitting as usual."

"Frog! It's not my fault if the guy they tortured didn't write down the exact zip code!"

"You're so not getting my money!"

The money! That totally kicks Malou back into gear. She shields her eyes with her hand, even though the sun's not even out, and peers into the far distance, like that's going to help.

"Give me a second, all right?" She points randomly eastward. "That's it. This way. I'd bet my wig on it."

"No, not that way," Zelda says, looking in the opposite direction and walking toward the riverbank. "We are on the wrong side of the river." She points across the Seine.

"How would you . . . oh."

On the other bank, across Pont de Sully, fire trucks, police cars, and ambulances are gathered in front of a burning building.

"You think they did this?"

"I know they did," Zelda confirms, heading toward the bridge. "Valks are very destructive."

"These girls are wild," Malou says, returning from interrogating the crowd around the burning building.

The entire neighborhood seems to have come down to the street to get a better look at the damage and show the firefighters their expensive Hermès nightgowns.

"They're talking about young girls breaking into every single apartment in the building looking for Johnny Depp and then setting the place on fire when they're done searching."

"Did they see them dragging out his body or a large bag that could contain it?" Zelda asks.

"No. No deal. You see, this proves once more that what you get for free is worthless." Malou winks at me. "The concierge was, like, freaking out. She was half-naked and screaming that Johnny doesn't live there anymore. He lives on a farm down south. He's there right now, and I know the place. It's near Saint-Tropez. So who's totally worth nine hundred fifty-two euros?"

Nine hundred fifty-two euros, my foot! "Wasn't he supposed to be at this party you were going to with Zelda tonight?"

"My information can't be a hundred percent accurate all the time, Frog. I know a lot of very unreliable people, you know."

"And this new piece of information is accurate because . . . ?"

"The poor concierge was practically exposing her boobs, screaming at the firefighter that Johnny is down south." She points toward the burning building. "That has to count for something."

"Bullshit!"

"He's in Saint-Tropez!"

"We don't know that!"

"You're so negative, Frog."

"You're so crazy, Malou!"

"What is Saint-Tropez?" Zelda asks, ignoring our bickering.

"It's a town waaaaay down south," I say, shaking my head. "It's like a gazillion hours' drive from here." I know because Édouard has a villa near Saint-Tropez, and we used to spend entire days getting asphyxiated on cigarette fumes while driving down there. "And we don't even have a car."

Zelda sighs. She checks the vanishing key marking on her arm. "We need a car," she says, looking around at all the parked ones as if we can take our pick.

"It's so funny you should say that!" Malou sneers, giving me an annoying, victorious side look. "According to everyone, the Valkies stole a car from someone who lives in that building and drove off looking for more stuff to burn."

––––––––––

Malou always says she loves me like the brother she never had—so why is she always putting me in these terrible situations?

Zelda said, "The Valks are doing everything right. Let's steal a car."

Malou said, "I don't know how to steal a car." She also said that she used to date a guy who stole cars for a living and that you can't just improvise—there's an art to it.

But then Malou turned to me and asked, "What about your mom's car, Frog?"

And Zelda said, "Yes, that's right. What about your mother's car?"

So I said, "Oh no, forget about it. The keys are inside our apartment."

And they both stared at me, like, well, no big deal then. You just need to go into your apartment and get the damn keys.

So I told them, "No way. I'm not going back there to steal Mom's car. She loves that car."

So Zelda said, "Do not force me to hurt you, dwarf," and that was the end of that discussion.

The lights are off in our apartment. I'm never too eager to go home, knowing Mom's in there, waiting to start yelling at me as soon as I walk through the door. But tonight, I really *can't* do it. I CAN'T. Just thinking about taking one more step toward the building is making me nauseous.

"She'll kill me if I go in there."

Malou disagrees. "She's probably totally zonked on sleeping pills. Go." She pushes me forward.

I resist. "What about your dad?"

Malou shakes her head. "Won't hear you. She yells at him so much he's practically deaf by now."

I turn to Zelda with imploring eyes. "Don't make me do this. Please!"

"Be courageous, Pudin," she says.

Sigh.

"Grab some food, too," Malou adds. "I'm starving. Get whatever's left of the caviar. And wine, if you can. Anything as long as it's white and chilled." She slaps my butt to encourage me. "Attaboy!"

I unlock the door and push it open very quietly. A thick cloud of filthy cigarette stench hits me in the face. I step in, leaving the door wide open to make sure I have a ready escape route.

So far, so good: Mom's car keys are just a few feet away in the crystal bowl on top of the hall table. I see them shining in the pale glow of streetlight coming through the French doors. All I need to do is take two, maybe three steps forward, grab them, and run.

A one, a two . . .

"Édouard, is that you?" Mom asks, coming out of her room.

Shit.

She switches on the hallway lights. "Oh, it's you." She leans against the wall. Malou was right about one thing: Mom's drugged up to her gills.

"Where's Édouard?" she asks vaguely.

She's wearing her thin white kimono and lingerie. She's put on way too much makeup, like a creepy geisha, something she does often when she swallows too many pills.

"I don't know," I answer. She probably gave him such hell tonight that he went to the hotel, like he does sometimes.

"I'm going to lie down," she says, but instead of going into her bedroom, she wanders into the living room and instinctively switches on all the lights. She probes around with her hands as if she's walking in the dark.

I grab the car keys. Now would be a good time to leave and let her be. I step back, but stop when she stumbles into the coffee table and falls flat on the floor.

"Édouard!" she calls.

"He's not here."

"Édouard, I fell. Help me," she whines.

Hesitantly, I walk into the living room and then squat in front of her, grab her hand, and help her to sit up. When she looks into my eyes, there's a spark of recognition in her strangely painted eyes. She slaps me really hard. One of her fingernails catches the inside corner of my nostril and *snap*!

I see stars: red ones, yellow ones, and some green ones, too. I take my hand off my nose. There's blood on my fingers, and I feel plenty more running down my face.

"It's . . . it's nothing, it was an accident," I tell Mom, doing my best to hide my bleeding nose. But the blood is just pouring out of me.

"Blood," Mom says, immediately trying to wipe off the drops that fall on her legs and fancy white kimono. She shows me her bloody palm like she doesn't understand what happened.

"Leave him alone!" Malou screams from behind me before grabbing me and dragging me away. When she sees the blood on my face, she goes ballistic. "Did you hit him, you *bitch*?"

"You!" Mom says when she sees Zelda entering the living room. "That's my black c—"

Zelda doesn't let her finish the sentence; she kneels in front of her, grabs her wrists, and sings the strange sleeping whale lullaby. Mom's head rolls back, and Zelda eases her body down on the carpet.

Malou approaches carefully. She probes her with her foot, checking her vital signs. "Well done, Zelda. You killed the ugly witch!"

Mom starts snoring to prove her wrong.

"Are you all right?" Malou asks, squatting in front of me.

"I'm fine. It was an accident," I mumble, wiping the blood away with the back of my hand.

"Let me see," Zelda says.

"It's just a scratch," I protest, but she examines it anyway—doctor's instinct, I guess.

"I'll let you lick his wounds," Malou says, walking away to get some food from the kitchen.

"We saw the lights." Zelda nods toward the French doors. "We thought you were in trouble." Her touch feels so gentle after Mom trying to snap off my nose.

"I was . . . I'm . . . I . . ." It's her hand on my face that does it. I do something incredibly stupid: I lean forward and hug her.

I can feel her body stiffening. She doesn't know how to deal with this embarrassing Earthling display of affection (EDA). Her own arms and hands stay a million miles away from me, and now that I'm so stupidly locked against her, I'm too ashamed to pull away and look into her eyes.

"Oops," I hear Malou say. I look up past Zelda's shoulder and see her coming out of the kitchen with a couple bottles of wine. "I'm going to, *you know* . . ." She starts retreating tactfully.

"No! You can stay," Zelda says, breaking away from me. "We were done. Your nose is fine."

But the rest of me wants to die.

05
EXPIRATION: 14 HOURS

The sun's rising on the highway. I don't feel like talking. No one feels like talking. We haven't said a single word since Malou drove Mom's car out of the garage.

Malou takes a swig of white wine. She says she's a better driver when she's drunk. She also says not speeding with a sports car is a crime. She tries to hand the bottle to Zelda. "It smoothes things out," she explains.

"What things?"

"Life."

"I could try some," I say.

"In your dreams, Frog!"

The cut on my nose hurts. I touch it.

"Don't touch it," Malou says, watching me in the rearview mirror.

"Why did you launch into physical contact?" Zelda asks suddenly.

"Physical contact?"

"After your mother cut your nose, you took me in your arms. I would like to know why, Earthling."

Malou spits a mouthful of wine back into the bottle. "Oh ho! Try explaining that one, Frog!"

Actually, I've been rehearsing a little speech in my head. "I didn't 'launch into physical contact.' I was upset because of my mother. You were there. And . . . well . . . that's all, really."

See? No big deal.

"Emotions again," Zelda says, shaking her head.

"Yeah, we Earthlings are completely rotten with them."

"If your mother is such a problem, why don't you just walk away?"

"My point exactly," Malou says.

"I will. One day, when I'm older."

"Zook says that to truly become yourself, you should kill your parents."

"Do you mean, like, *literally*?" Malou asks, suddenly very interested in Zookism.

"No, Zook means symbolically."

Symbolically killing one's parents is way less interesting to Malou. "The first religion that says it's all right to kill my dad, I'm signing on," she says.

Malou goes back to drinking and driving. Zelda goes back to staring at the horizon, as if she's trying to spot the three Vahalalians ahead of us. I go back to feeling bad about hugging her.

"We need more wine." Malou shows us the nearly empty bottle. "And we need to stop at a gas station to fill the tank."

"So did they," Zelda says, pointing toward a black column of smoke rising in the distance. The Valks played with matches again.

Malou slows down.

GAS STATION, NEXT EXIT, the road sign says.

I glue my face against the window to get a better look at the result of the Valks' favorite activity: burning down the house.

Firefighters are running around the gas station like headless chickens, desperately spraying water all over the burning building. Police cars are strewn everywhere, some burning or upside down.

"It looks like a battlefield," I say, now switching to the rear window to get a last glance at the mess the Valks have left behind.

Something roars above us. I open my window to look up. Three police helicopters shoot forward, following the deserted highway line.

"Those Valks are a blast!" Malou says, and sucks the last drop of wine out of the bottle.

Boom! The gas station blows away in a mushroom of black smoke and red-orange flames to illustrate her point.

Another fire blazes straight ahead on the highway. This time they used two police cars as fuel. One is belly-up; the other, just burning peacefully in the middle of the road.

Malou slows down and zigzags carefully between the two burning wrecks. I turn to the side of the road. A couple shell-shocked policemen are desperately crawling away on all fours.

"Should we, like, help them or something?" I ask.

"No, we help *her*," Zelda says.

Her *who*? But then I see her—the fury the policemen are trying to get away from. She's wobbling in the middle of the road in some sort of desperate war stance, ready to take on the next police car to show up at her little police-smacking party. She's Tena or Lela or Pela—one of them—looking like she's been run over by a truck or two, her face and hair covered in blood and dirt, her clothes burned in places.

But as the saying goes, *you should see the other guys*.

Malou stops the car right in front of her.

"I'll get her," Zelda says, opening her door.

"*Get* her?" I have a much better plan. "Let's drive *over* her! Or at least drive *around* her and get the hell out of here."

Zelda gives me a dirty look. "You should overcome your cowardice, Pudin." And she climbs out of the car.

Ha. Me? *Overcome my cowar—*

"Wait!" I call after her.

Zelda turns to me, looking annoyed. "What?"

"Where is she going to sit?"

"There in the back, next to you."

Like I should have no problem with that. "I don't want her beside me. Did you see the kind of damage she can do with that baton?"

"There's no fight left in her, can't you see?"

Oh, *sorry* for not noticing when a Vahalalian Valk is not in serial-killer mode anymore.

Zelda lifts the Valk and gently sets her down in the backseat. Oh God. Look at all the blood and soot on the creamy leather of Mom's car!

"Which one is this?" I ask, trying to sit as far away as possible.

"That is Lena," Zelda answers.

"There's blood coming out of her ears!" I shriek.

Sometimes it's just difficult for a regular Pudin to overcome cowardice.

"What happened at the station?" Zelda asks calmly.

"They gave us trouble. We gave them trouble back." Lena stops to cough up some blood.

"What about your friends?" I ask.

"One stays behind, two go forward," she mutters.

We all look to the left of the highway. The three police helicopters are flying in circles over the forest. Looks to me like the competition is blocked in there for good and we're going to take a serious lead in the race to Johnny.

I turn to Lena to see what she thinks about that. "Omigod! She's dead!" I poke her arm, and she collapses against the door like a bleeding bag of potatoes.

Zelda leans over the seat to check her pulse. Lena opens her eyes. They're like two big white balls against a sooty black background.

"*Squiiik squiiiik, squikiti squik*," she whispers, trying to sit up. Zelda helps her.

I'm sorry to be so materialistic at such a highly dramatic moment, but now the entire door is covered in blood and tar!

"*Squiiiikiti squiiik*," continues Lena, looking at Zelda with a strange intensity.

"What is she saying?" I ask.

"She just met Zook," Zelda translates.

"Zook talked about Zelda," Lena whispers. "She said she needs to go into the forest and save my sisters."

"Ha. How convenient," I sneer. "Did Zook say we should take your baton and beat ourselves over the head?"

"Shut up, Pudin." Zelda gives me a nasty push on the shoulder. "What else did she say?" She turns back to Lena, cupping her face in her hand and forcing her to focus.

"She said you've been struggling with sinful thoughts. She said you shouldn't be scared. She said sometimes you need to do something very wrong to accomplish something very good. Zook said she will always protect you and be with you, Zelda."

"What does that mean?" I ask.

"It means stop the car!" Zelda shouts.

"What?!"

"You heard her. Zook asked me to rescue the Vahalalians."

Crap! "She's lying!"

"Vahalalians don't lie."

Okay, let's change strategy: "Zelda. There will be, like, a gazillion policemen in that forest, and they all think you're a menace to society, an arsonist, and a cop hater."

"He's right," Malou agrees. "The cops always get jumpy when you start kicking their own kind. Especially since you're a girl and all that."

"It won't matter," Zelda says, grabbing Lena's baton and warming up for combat by smashing it against multiple invisible heads. "Zook will protect me."

I wish they had invented skepticism on Vahalal.

———

I don't completely freak out until Malou stops the car at the very end of a dirt road, right at the edge of the forest, and I hear dogs barking madly.

No one said anything about dogs.

"Dogs!" I say. "Let's drive away before it's too late!"

But Zelda has another plan. "You all stay in the car," she says. "I'll bring them back." And—*zoom*—she's heading toward the forest all alone.

I jump out of the car and try to follow her. "Dogs, Zelda!" I say as if it were totally self-explanatory.

She doesn't stop. She doesn't say "Oh yes, dogs and armed policemen, helicopters flying over our heads. You are totally right,

David. Let's forget about this and go get some sun in Saint-Tropez." No, she just hangs Mom's coat on the barbed-wire fence edging the forest and jumps over.

I'm sure the policemen are going to have a fit just seeing her swinging a baton in a vintage Paco Rabanne swimsuit.

"What if they catch you?" I call after her. She stops and turns to me. I swear she even smiles. "They'll never catch me, Pudin. The forest is my favorite combat field."

I feel a pressure point on my chest as she disappears in the vegetation. "She's gone," I say to no one in particular, and retrieve Mom's coat from the fence, doing my best not to tear it on the barbed wire.

I walk back to the car, squeezing the coat against me. I look up and freeze.

Holy spaghetti! Police cars are driving up the dirt road, blocking all possible exits. Malou gets out of the car. "What are we going to do, Frog?"

Lena opens the car door and stumbles out, knowing exactly what we should do. "Run! To the forest!"

Despite her injuries, she grabs Malou's arm and pushes her toward the fence. "Come on!" she yells at me.

"I can't go in there," I plead. And since she doesn't seem to get my point, I explain it as simply as I can: "Dogs!!!" Barking, yapping, ready-to-bite-juvenile-delinquent-butt dogs.

She comes back and grabs my arm, too, dragging me toward the forest like she did with Malou. "You will die fighting, Earthling!"

Is that her idea of a pep talk?

16
EXPIRATION: 13 HOURS

I'm nothing like Zelda. Or Tena, Lena, or Pela. The forest will never be my favorite combat field. I fall on my knees and scratch my hands on the spiky undergrowth. I try to stand back up, but the thick, wet ground sucks me down and I slide backward on a slope of dead leaves and mud.

"Come on, Frog. You're slowing us down," Malou shouts back at me.

"Wait for me!" I call desperately. What can I say? I don't have the right physique to be running away from the police.

When I look up, I don't see Malou or this Lena Supergirl anywhere. It's so damn humiliating on top of everything else. "Malou!" I call.

"*Woof woof,*" the dogs answer for her.

I'm panting so hard, I expect to spit out a lung any minute.

"There, boys, there. Catch!" I hear a voice shout far behind me. Oh, crap, crap, crap!

I told you already. Rottweiler. German shepherd. Freaking house poodle like Pipette. I just don't like dogs.

I go for a desperate final sprint uphill, and all I can hear is those dogs panting and galloping after me. I feel a paw first, like the dogs are poking me and teasing me, and—*SLAM!*—a shooting pain jolts my calves before I fall flat on the ground.

I roll my body into a ball and the dogs gather for the feast. They work on my arms. My butt. My legs. My skull. They're eating me alive!

"Let him go, boys, let him go," a man shouts.

The dogs yelp as the policemen pull them away from me. A thousand hands grab me and rough me up. "Where do you think you were running, you little shit?"

"Hey, easy with him," someone more considerate says. A policeman lifts me to my feet. "He's just a kid."

The dogs yelp even harder: "A kid? Damn it! We love eating kids!"

———————

I check my leg and rub the bruise. Oh boy. I don't want to end up in a juvenile prison—with my height and good looks, I bet it's not going to be like summer camp.

They lock me in the back of a police van parked with the rest of their armada at the other side of the forest and tell me that my friends will join me soon. They sound pretty confident about that. They also tell me I'm in plenty of trouble and, by the looks of it, I have to agree with them.

I tell you. These policemen really hate us. They gave me plenty of dirty looks while they dragged me into the van, and they have only nasty things to say about Zelda. I wish they would call Dad. Dad's a champion at handling angry cops and defending bad kids.

The back door of the van opens. A man comes in. He nods at me, and I recognize him: He's the bald policeman from Cornouaille. The one who chased us on the roof. He looks a bit different with two blackened eyes, a bruised face, and a broken nose hidden under a large bandage.

He's holding two plastic cups and hands me one. "Hot chocolate," he says rather gently. I take it. He takes a sip of his coffee. I take a sip of my hot chocolate. "Quite a mess, huh?"

"Yes," I agree.

"I was just talking with your dad on the phone. He's in a lot of trouble because of you."

We sip together.

"She's quite a girl, isn't she?" he says.

"You have no idea," I whisper, looking down at my Converse.

"If I were your age, I'd do all sorts of crazy things to impress her. You know what I mean?"

I nod. We sip.

"This is going to end in tears if you don't help us stop her." His voice is a little nasal because of his broken nose. "The boys are getting anxious, and when the boys get anxious, they make mistakes. You know what I'm talking about?"

The boys = the policemen, and I have bruises and bites all over my body to help me get his point.

"Any idea where she could be hiding, David?"

He stares straight into my eyes. It takes superhuman power to say, "I don't know."

He shakes his head, like I'm a total disappointment. I'm about to take another sip of the chocolate, but he slaps the cup out of my hands.

"Look what I've done now."

Yeah, look. There's hot chocolate all over the van, and my fingers hurt so much I need to squeeze them under my armpits.

"I have another question for you, David. But this time I'd like a straight answer." He puts his coffee cup down, probably in case he decides to slap me some more. "Why is she after Johnny Depp?"

I can't answer that. If I did, it would make things worse.

"Your fingers hurt?"

My throat gets tight, but I'd rather die than cry in front of him. "If you smack me again," I say with a trembling voice, "I'll tell my dad. He gets people like you fired all the time."

He sighs. "Who's smacking who, *huh*?" he says, picking up both cups from the floor. "I'm taking you back to Paris to see if your famous dad can beat some answers out of you."

He's wrong. Mom's the real smacker in the family.

————————

He sits me down in his car, buckles my seat belt. There, all cozy for the ride home. He waves at the other policemen before driving away.

"There's something I want to ask you," he says as we drive off. "When we were on that roof, you know, did you see . . . anything *strange*?"

Here we go. "Like what?"

He clears his throat and sucks a cigarette out of his pack. "She was . . . you know . . . like . . . she was beside you and . . . then . . . she was . . . ." He can't find the right words to describe what he witnessed.

"Forget about it," he finally says, lighting the cigarette.

"Space Splash," I mumble hesitantly.

"What did you just say?"

"The ability to be at two points in space at the same time. That's how she . . . *you know*." I nod toward his broken nose.

He turns to me as if I actually poked it. "You think you're so smart, you little shit?"

See? They just get more upset when you tell them the plain truth.

"Do you know how this little adventure is going to end, David?"

I look him straight in the eye. "My money's on Johnny Depp departing Earth for a very long intergalactic vacation."

He pokes my forehead with the two fingers holding his cigarette. "She's going to mess up your head so bad, even your famous dad isn't going to be able to fix you."

I try to open my window, but it's locked.

"What happened on the roof . . ." He shakes his head. He really doesn't like thinking about the roof episode. "I know what's real. And I know what's fantasy. And you, kid, you're lost in a fantasy."

"Can you open my window?" I ask.

He presses a button and my window rolls down. "I'll tell you how it's going to end: When she's done using you, she'll abandon you, and you'll end up in a padded cell telling everyone your Space-girl story."

"Go to hell," I say, looking away. "Get a wig!"

He actually laughs. "That's a funny one, kid," he says, looking in his rearview mirror. He turns around. "That's odd."

I turn around to see what's so odd. A police car is catching up and flashing its signal lights at us. The bald guy presses a few keys on his car radio. "Why don't they use the radio?" he says, stopping our car in the emergency lane.

The police car stops right behind us. I look more carefully and see the driver waving at me from behind the wheel. It's not a police-man at all. It's Malou!

Three doors open at once. Pela, Tena, Zelda, and whatever is left of Lena come out of the police car, all of them looking exhausted, worn out, and beaten down but ready to kick some more police butt.

I get out of the car just in time to see the bald man turn white. "Damn," he whispers. He puts his hand on his service gun. Zelda shakes her head. Uh-uh. I don't think so, pal.

"Oh no, not again," he whines.

Yes, again. She does her thing: Space Splash! *Poof*, she reappears right beside him, her baton raised above his head.

She slams. His bandage flies away, and he falls like a sack of soup. Sleep tight.

"You're all right?" Zelda asks, putting away the baton.

I think of all the dog bites and my burned fingers, but then I nod. I am rather all right. Actually, I'm freaking great now that SHE'S BACK!

"Tadpole!" Malou jumps out of the car and sprints to me with the velocity of a torpedo. *Boom!* She squeezes me senseless.

"How did you get a police car?" I ask when she stops frenetically kissing my face.

She dries her tears. "Not peacefully, I tell you. Those girls have real issues with violence."

"Let's move," Zelda says coldly, bringing us back to business. She walks away. I run to catch up and walk silently beside her until I find the strength to tell her why my heart is racing. "You came back for me."

"No." She points at Malou. "She's the one who insisted that we get you back."

"Like hell I did!" Malou shrieks. "The minute she realized you didn't make it, she became hysterical. She was, like, *Where is my pudding? Where did they take my pudding? We need to get my pudding back!*"

I turn to the other Vahalalians. They frown suggestively: She really was.

"Ha. You two are so funny," Malou says, laughing. "Come on, *Zeldie*," she calls after her. "Just give him a hug."

"Enough, Earthlings!" Zelda shouts, getting in the car. She slams the door behind her.

"Ooh la la. Touchy!" Malou winks at me and pinches my arm exactly where it hurts. "I'm so not buying her Ice Bitch Princess act anymore. She totally has a crush on you!"

I feel strange walking to the car. Strange and terribly happy. Because I know there's some truth to what Malou just said. I sit right beside Zelda. Malou starts the engine and drives away. No one talks. Everyone stares at the road ahead.

I do something incredibly courageous. Probably the most courageous thing I will ever do in my life. I search for Zelda's hand and take it in mine without any hesitation. I don't need to look at her to know that she's all right with that. She just squeezes my hand back. And I feel like the happiest creature in the entire universe.

17

EXPIRATION: 3 HOURS

We all used to go to the villa together, Mom, Édouard, Malou, and I. That was a long time ago, before they kicked Malou out and started sending me to Cornouaille for the summers.

I love the villa. It has a swimming pool with a wooden deck and a terrace that gives you a view all the way to the Saint-Tropez bay. There's a large olive tree with a swing. I used to spend hours on that swing.

There's always black currant sorbet in the freezer in the pool house. Every time I taste something with black currant flavor, I think of summertime, Malou, and swimming pools.

The villa is just a few miles away from Saint-Tropez in a fancy-pants lot of villas called Beauvallon. Édouard's so proud to own here. Normally, only celebrities and absurdly rich people can own a villa in Beauvallon. Édouard is not a celebrity, and he is definitely not absurdly rich (Mom's the big earner). He just inherited the villa from his parents.

———

Pela drops us off in front of the villa. She's going to hide the police car far away. We climb over the gate as she drives away.

"I didn't remember it being so small," I say, walking toward the main building.

In my memory, Édouard's villa is like a bright white castle surrounded by a park, not this little gray bungalow in the middle of a messy little garden. There's no swing in the olive tree anymore, and the tree is actually so small, I don't see how it ever could have carried a swing anyway.

"I can't believe it. Even the swimming pool has shrunk." To be honest, it's just a glamorized bathtub, empty and filled with dead leaves.

"Everything always looks better in memories," Malou says, getting the pool house keys from a loose brick in the wall.

She goes to get the main house keys from inside the liquor cabinet, and I check the freezer in the pool house. It's turned off, totally empty, and smells stuffy. No black currant sorbet. How horribly disappointing.

———————

It's Vahalalian opera night in the living room. As dozens of African statues and masks from Édouard's collection gaze down from the walls, Tena and Pela take turns singing to Lena while Malou lounges on the gigantic white sofa by the old fireplace, emptying a bottle of rosé wine. "This is better than a rave," she says, closing her eyes and moving her hands to the strange melody.

"Quiet!" orders Pela, taking her turn singing.

I leave them to it and go to find Zelda. She has set up camp in my old room. The door is wide open. She sits on the bare mattress like a sexy Buddha, her legs crossed lotus style, her eyes closed, her palms turned skyward. I feel like I'm disturbing something and try to walk away silently.

"We're back where we started," she says without even opening her eyes. "You're staring at me strangely, and I still don't know why."

She opens her eyes. They're still beautifully green, but maybe not quite so mean.

"What were you doing? You looked like you were meditating." I walk hesitantly into the room. The walls are still covered with large framed posters of my favorite Marvel heroes: Wolverine, Nova, the Silver Surfer.

"I was praying to Zook," she says. "I'm trying to understand what she wants from me." She gets up from the bed and takes a step toward me.

"Do you want me to leave?"

She puts her hands on my shoulders. "I'm done. I've already made up my mind."

"About what?"

She smiles faintly and checks her key tattoo. "About this."

"What about it?" I get closer to see for myself. You can hardly see it now.

"I believe Zook wants me to wait a bit longer," she says calmly, like running out of time and fading tattoos are no longer burning issues.

"How?"

She looks up at me. "You'll know in time."

"You're so cryptic."

"You look so tense."

Is it me, or is the space between us reducing at breakneck speed?

"I . . . well . . . you . . . um . . ."

I have totally forgotten why I came to see her and what I wanted to ask her.

"What?" she asks.

Oh, I remember: "There's a place I want to show you." I take her hands off my shoulders and pull her gently toward the panel window.

She resists a little. "We cannot go out, Pudin. We will be seen."

"It's going to be all right, I promise," I say, pulling up the blinds and opening the sliding window. I look up at the sky. I love this time of day at Édouard's villa. The sun's gone, but there will still be hours of dreamy, warm blue twilight.

She follows me to the terrace hesitantly, looking around for possible spies.

"All we have to do is run across the garden and into the woods." I point at the pine trees on the other side of the empty swimming pool. "Once we're in the woods, it's like we're invisible."

She studies the garden and then nods. Okay, we're on.

We run silently along the swimming pool and slide down a small slope into the woods. We land on the path left by a dried-up river. She stops to look at the beautiful surroundings and closes her eyes to smell the air: sun-baked ground, pine trees, and the sea. The insects are buzzing their own opera around us. The crickets go at it wildly in the warmth. You can hear kids laughing and splashing in the swimming pool of the nearby campground. If I wanted to stage this whole scene, I couldn't make it any better.

"This way," I say, taking her hand and leading her down to the dry riverbed. The path leads to a place that's out of this world. My own dreamland. I push a last pine branch out of our way, and we're on the beach. Unlike the house, this is exactly the way I remember it. A tiny stretch of white sand cut off from the rest of the bay by a thick layer of pines and bushes.

I sit down on the warm sand and point at the sea. "Ta-da!"

"Why are we here?" Zelda asks.

I spent my entire childhood dreaming of this—bringing someone special down here to share my loot of black currant sorbet. "Isn't it beautiful? I love this place. It's probably my favorite place in the world."

"What do you do here?"

"You rest. You lie on the sand. You dream. You . . . you swim, of course! Don't you like swimming?"

She shakes her head. "All nonsubterranean bodies of liquid on Vahalal will either melt you or boil you. We don't swim."

"What about nonmelting, nonboiling swimming pools?"

"Water is holy for us. It's a sin to use it for leisure."

"Zelda! Here comes another Earthling treat! Maybe even better than vanilla ice cream." I peel off my T-shirt and start unlacing my sneakers. "And since you always walk around in a swimsuit, all you really have to do is kick off those boots."

"Your body," she says when I stand up wearing nothing but my boxer shorts.

"Yeah, I know." I shrug helplessly. "I'm too skinny, right?" But that's nothing she hasn't seen before.

"It's not that," she says, reaching for my hips and touching a bruise.

"Oh. The dogs," I say, tensing under her touch. "I hate dogs."

She grabs my hand and twists my arm to get a better look at the other dog bites on my arm. She presses and squeezes one of the bruises.

"OUCH!"

"Does it hurt?"

"Only when you pinch it!"

She laughs! I've never heard her laugh before.

"Where else did they bite you?"

"On my head."

She pulls me to her. She twists my neck, bends my head in all the directions of the compass—south, north, east, west—looking for the bites. A mother gorilla searching for lice wouldn't put less heart into it. When she's done looking, she *launches into physical contact*, hugging me really tight.

I put my arms around her. That's it. Nothing can ever break us apart. Until . . . she pushes me away hard, and I fall on the sand. She grabs a piece of driftwood, getting into her war stance and turning toward the riverbed.

A group of little kids stands there silently. They all have wet hair. They're all wearing swimsuits. They all have this expression, like, "What are you doing on our secret beach with your pants down?"

"They're just kids, Zelda," I say, standing up and taking the piece of driftwood away from her before she decides to Space Splash it in their faces. I throw it back into the sea and pick up my clothes and shoes.

The kids get out of Zelda's way as she pushes a branch aside and walks back up to the path. I put my T-shirt back on and follow her. I stop midway to put on my pants and shoes. The kids are following us silently. I slowly lace up my Converse ultras, waiting for the kids to go away. They finally disappear into the woods toward the campground.

I turn toward Édouard's villa. Zelda's gone. I wonder if she's furious about what happened down on the beach. Or if she's just like me, wishing those kids had never come to interrupt us. "Next time, we swim!" I say to myself, running along the path to catch up with her.

———————

We're finishing dinner at the kitchen table. Spaghetti and canned tomatoes à la Malou. I haven't talked with Zelda since the beach incident. I slurp my spaghetti, trying to make eye contact with her, wondering if she's mad at me.

"I don't like this place," Tena says, helping herself to more pasta.

"It's really beautiful when the blinds are open," I say, grabbing the platter from her.

The Valks won't let us open the blinds to air out the house. They don't care about the stuffy atmosphere, the sea, or the spectacular views at dawn. They only care about the surrounding geography and the absence of a good escape route in the event of a police raid.

"This house is a trap," confirms Pela. "Reminds me of the time we got cornered in that whorehouse during the Babylonian wars."

"What a beautiful bloodbath!" reminisces Tena, licking her fork. "Remember that big guy? What was his name? Ugo something. He used to wear human heads on a necklace."

"Ugo the Chopper. He had this trick with two axes." Pela demonstrates with her fork and spoon. Chop! "He would cut off a head in one single, neat move. Even the mother liked him."

"She was different back then." Lena uses her fingers to scrape up the sauce left on her plate. "She could still appreciate a male if he had a talent for mass murder."

"Those were the days," Tena agrees, pushing her empty plate away. "Good pasta, by the way."

"Thanks. And thanks for all the heartwarming head-chopping stories." Malou stands up, looking exhausted. "I'm going to rest my eyes a little," she says, leaving the table. "By the way, Zeldie, you'll find plenty of clean swimsuits in the master bedroom. And regular clothes, too." She walks out to the terrace like a zombie. She's going to sleep in the pool house. She always used to claim it as hers, once upon a time.

"There are plenty of other bedrooms if you want to sleep," I tell the rest of the gang.

The Valks leave the table and Tena and Pela help Lena walk out of the kitchen.

Zelda and I are completely alone. Everything is quiet except for the buzzing in my head.

"I'm sorry for what happened down there." I point vaguely toward the secret beach. "It was totally my fault. I shouldn't have dragged you there."

She shrugs, like it doesn't matter, and looks at me from across the table. She smiles faintly. "Come here, Pudin."

"Why?"

"Unfinished protocol."

I carefully walk around the table. She's way less careful. She grabs my T-shirt, drags me down, kisses the top of my head. Then the tip of my nose. Then my lips.

The bald guy with the broken nose was right: I'm losing my mind for her. And I don't care if it means having my eyes turned into black balls, blowing up like a water balloon, or being changed into a singing donkey. "I'm crazy about you, Zelda," I whisper, kissing her back.

She's not listening. She's all action and no words. She stands up and drags me to the living room, still kissing me. She reaches for the sofa and snatches the wolf fur blanket Mom likes so much, then puts it around us and pulls me down to the floor.

I'm about to speak again. She doesn't want me to.

"Quiet," she says. "Listen to me."

Silence.

"Sometimes you need to do something very wrong to accomplish something very good," she says.

Silence.

"When you'll wake up, I'll be gone."

———————

"Where's Zelda?" Malou asks, coming into the living room and scratching her messy hair. She's wearing one of Édouard's long-sleeve shirts as pajamas. "Where's everyone else?"

It's early morning. You can see a deep blue sky through the skylights. The sun will be up any minute. Everyone's gone. The Valks. Zelda. It's just me and Malou left.

"I don't know. Leave me alone."

"Why did you sleep on the floor?" Malou asks, squatting beside me. "Wait a second. Are you, like, *naked* under there?" She lifts the fur blanket and takes a peek. "Omigod! You're totally naked!"

I snatch the blanket back.

She gives me a wary sidelong look. "What did I miss, Tadpole?"

"Zelda's gone."

"Gone *where*?"

"I don't know. Can you let me sleep now?"

I turn my back to her. Zelda abandoned me while I was sleeping. I woke up, searched for her. Waited an eternity. Now I'm sure she's not coming back under that blanket. The world can crumble. I don't care.

"What did you guys do?"

"Nothing!"

"Did you . . . ?"

"Mind your own business."

"Taaadpole!"

"Stop calling me that! I'm not a kid anymore."

"Oh, I see. You're a *man* now." She grabs my arm. "What's that?"

"What?"

"That! On your arm!"

I look at the inside of my left arm.

"Is that a freaking *tattoo*?" Malou yells.

"I don't know. It's . . ." I can't believe it. There's a black triangular octopus proudly holding a stick on my arm! It's the key—the same tattoo that was vanishing on Zelda's arm. I try to brush it off, but it's deep under my skin, the sharp black edge all red and irritated.

"Did she give *this thing* to you the way she said you give it to people?" Malou holds my arm, inspecting it closely.

"I think so."

"You think so? Tadpole! Sex with a Spacegirl! Tattoos! What's wrong with you?"

"Nothing's wrong with me. Leave me alone!"

I can't stand Malou anymore. I can't stand myself, either. I reach for my clothes, throw off the fur blanket, and shoot for the bathroom. At least there's a lock on the door and I can be alone in there.

"Nice butt, lover," Malou calls after me.

———————

A cold shower doesn't help. Banging my head against the freezing tiled wall is just marginally better.

Why did she do that? Why did she give me the key and then leave? The more I try to wash it off, the redder it gets. Is this some sort of sick Vahalalian trick? A stupid souvenir that will remind me of her forever?

Like I need a freaking tattoo for that.

Malou knocks on the door. "What are we going to do without Zelda?"

If only I could have another attack of Eol-69 and be done with it! I stick out my tongue and check it in the mirror. It's never been pinker.

"David! Let me in!" *Bang bang bang!*

I stop the water, snatch a towel, cover myself with it, and lie down in the cold bathtub. I plan to disappear into a cocoon and never ever reappear.

"Don't leave me alone," Malou begs. "The phone's ringing. David!"

I put my hands over my ears. I close my eyes. The pain just won't go. It's everywhere in me.

"I hear something in the garden. Frog! Please open the door."

What have I done? Why did she have to go? Will she ever come back? Why couldn't she stay with me? Why does everything have to be so painful?

"There's someone at the door."

"Zelda," I say, passing my fingers over the weird symbol on my arm, "why did you give me the key?"

"Omigod. They're coming in. Get out of there, David! We need to—"

Then Malou's gone. Then they break down the door. Then they drag me and my cocoon out of the tub.

And then I don't care.

08

KEY TO VAHALAL LOCKED ON THE EARTHLING CREATURE CALLED DAVID GERSHWIN— VALIDITY: UNLIMITED

"**D**o you believe you were the instrument of a higher power?"

The Red Tie Man waits for an answer, tap-tapping his pencil on his questionnaire.

"Can you repeat the question?" Malou asks, frowning.

"Are you responsible for your own actions?" he repeats, pronouncing each word carefully.

I look up at his old, wrinkled face. I'm pretty sure this man hasn't smiled in at least two decades.

"David?" he asks me.

Forget about me. I'm not even here.

"I'm not sure what you mean," Malou says, trying to read his questionnaire upside down. "Is there, like, a right and wrong answer to that?"

"This person you were after, the actor, Johnny Depp." The Red Tie Man makes a face, like mentioning a celebrity is filthy. "He could press charges against you. Sue you and your parents. He could make you miserable. Do you realize that?"

Ha. Make my life miserable. Get in line!

"Are we, like, going to jail?" Malou asks.

The man sighs and brushes imaginary crumbs from his red tie. He's not an old policeman. He's an old therapist working for the police. We're not in a sinister interrogation room in a sinister police station; we're in a sinister interrogation room in a sinister juvenile nuthouse near Paris.

The Red Tie Man is trying to establish how deeply Zelda has messed up our sanity. He moves on to the next question: "Do you realize Zelda put your life and the lives of others in great danger? David? Can you answer that for me?"

Okay, I'll answer that for him. "Go to hell!"

He clears his throat and checks a box with his pencil. The "go to hell" box, I suppose.

"I bet you that wasn't the right answer," Malou whispers to me.

———

The Red Tie Man sends me back to my cell. There's a metal net over the window to remind me I'm a dangerous nutcase in a nutcase prison.

A bed, a toilet, a sink, four gray walls. Very minimal, just the way Mom would like it.

They gave me the excessively large and worn-out type of clothes Zelda was wearing the first time I saw her. I have slippers for shoes.

The door is locked. Zelda's out there somewhere. I want to be with her. I'm not. I'm dead.

Someone unlocks the door, and Dad comes in. I don't move. I stay quietly crouched on my bed, hugging my legs even tighter. I'm not even sure I'm happy to see him.

Dad's going to do all he possibly can to prove that *my* Zelda was just a daydream. I don't want her to become a daydream. I want Zelda to be Zelda.

There's no chair in my room, so he sits on the toilet. "I just talked with the judge," he says.

Dad's a real ace at looking poised when everything's crumbling around us. "So far, he's refusing to let me take Marie-Louise and you under my care."

Dad's about the only person in the world who calls Malou Marie-Louise. He doesn't believe in nicknames.

"Did they abuse you physically?"

"No."

"Did they imply you were crazy?"

I shrug.

"Don't let them tell you you're crazy. You are not crazy. You hear me?"

"Did she get him?" I ask.

"Who?"

"Johnny Depp. Did Zelda get him?"

Dad gets off the toilet and sits beside me on the bed. "Would it matter to you if she did?"

That's it, he's in child therapist mode.

"If she got him, I'll never see her again."

"Why do you think that?"

"Because she will take him to her planet, and she will never come back to Earth."

Dad seems to think about this. "David?"

"Yes."

"Try not to talk to anyone about Zelda until I get that order from the judge."

I'm not crazy—no, no—but other, less *understanding* people might think otherwise.

"She got him, then?"

"No, she never got to him. He's not even in France. He's away somewhere promoting his movies. It's . . ." Dad's looking for the right words. "You know, I believe this actor . . . what's his name . . . the pirate."

"Johnny Depp."

Dad nods. "He is not the real issue here."

"You're wrong. She's obsessed with him." She would stop at nothing, not even breaking my heart—or killing me, which is the same thing.

"No, David. She doesn't really want him. She's never even met him. He's just a name she put over her real purpose."

"What purpose?"

"Zelda is just like anyone else. Like you or like me. She wants exactly what we want."

"What's that?"

"To love someone and be loved back."

————

A young girl, also wearing worn-out, oversize clothes, brings me my dinner tray. "The food here sucks. It's freaking revolting," she says, leaving the tray beside me on the bed. "My name's Suzy, by the way. Suzy for Suzanne."

She drops a folded piece of paper on my lap when the male nurse isn't looking. "Don't worry, I'm cool. You're cute, but I'm not coming on to you. It's from your sister."

When they're gone, I unfold the note. It reads, "Hello, my little tadpole. Or is it 'Mister Man,' now that you're all clued up? How's life in your part of the nuthouse? I'm surrounded by totally crazy girls. Never felt so much at home. Ha ha ha! You can write back to me and give the note to Suzy. She's cool, but she probably told you that. She's here because she's a nymphomaniac, and since you're a sex beast, I'm sure you're going to love each other. Did you get any new tattoos? Write to me. I love you (like a sister, you perverted boy!)."

I stuff the piece of paper in my pocket. This is new. I never thought I'd miss Malou so much. It's good I don't have anything to write with, because if I did I wouldn't be able to resist the impulse to tell her I love her, too.

———————

I'm not myself anymore.

Before Zelda, I was a shy, obedient boy.

"Your father is making quite a ruckus to stop us from helping you," the Red Tie Man says.

I shrug. My father is a great therapist. This man is just a glamorized prison warden.

I'm meeting him in his office, one on one. The door's locked. A male nurse is waiting for me in the corridor outside the office, since I'm a dangerous loony.

"When you think of Zelda, how do you feel?"

I scratch the key tattoo. It's very itchy. I wonder if there are any side effects to it—like rage and the desire to strangle people with their red ties.

"Do you still believe she came from another planet?"

Before Zelda, I was a stupid Earthling like the Red Tie Man. Ignorant and weak. Since she transferred the key to me, I feel part Vahalalian.

"Should I take your silence as a yes?"

I shrug.

"Do you remember when you started to believe she was really from another planet?"

I have an answer for him this time. "When she started beating up people like you. That was totally out of this world."

The Red Tie Man is very sensitive. He cuts our session short and sends me back to my room.

The second the male nurse opens the door and pushes me into my cell, I smell trouble: Chanel No. 5 and menthol cigarette smoke.

MOM!

She sits on my bed, wearing purple-tinted bug-eye glasses, her legs crossed, waiting for me.

"You can't smoke in here," the male nurse tells her.

She drags on her cigarette dramatically. "Why don't you go wipe some ass somewhere else?" she tells him, and flicks the cigarette into the toilet.

She sounds lethally pissed off. I'm lethally pissed off, too. Let's get ready to rumble.

"For once, your father and I agree on one thing: My son doesn't belong in a nuthouse. You belong in your room, where you will be locked for the rest of your teen years." She taps on the bed beside her. "Come and sit here."

I don't move.

"Now!" she orders.

I shake my head to let her know I won't. This is new, too: I'm not scared of her anymore.

"I care for you, David. More than I care for anyone else. More than I care for myself."

"More than you care for your stupid black coat? Your car? Or the gazillion-dollar vase we broke?"

She sighs and closes her eyes. I'm sure she's struggling not to yell and scratch my face off, thinking of all her beloved items that we destroyed. "It was a *very nice coat*, you know." She takes off her purple-tinted bug-eye glasses. "But yes, I care for you marginally more than I care for that stupid coat or that vase."

She lights another cigarette. Drags nervously. "You should have seen how my parents treated me," she sneers. "Ha! Do you think they cared about me? Do you think they spoiled me like I spoil you? Though I didn't go stealing cars and burning down gas stations to upset them."

I take a few steps toward her. I'm going to do something I should have done years ago. I can see a mix of surprise and apprehension in her eyes as I get closer and lean over her. She probably knows I'm going to hug her. But before I do that, I grab the cigarette and throw it in the toilet. *Psssst*, it whispers before dying.

"I hate when you smoke," I say, and before she can start screaming, I wrap my arms around her. I rest my head against her chest. I feel her arms going around me. Hesitantly at first, then firmly.

She breathes deeply, squeezing me against her for the first time in a very long while. "I hate the terrible influence this crazy girl has on you," she says, her voice breaking.

We break apart. She quickly puts her glasses back on to hide that she's crying. She looks up at me and seems to notice something. "David?"

She stands up as if she just saw a ghost standing beside me. She grabs my arm. "What's THIS on your arm?" She lifts her glasses to get a better look at it. Oh, she's not crying anymore. "Is that a . . . a . . . a . . . ?"

I retreat into my cocoon. My arm hurts where Mom squeezed it. She screamed so much the male nurse rushed in to take her out of my room. She threatened to sue the nuthouse. She threatened to sue whoever put this "monstrosity" on my arm. But mostly she threatened to scratch the thing off with a butcher knife as soon as I'm back in her custody.

At dinner, Suzy has no new note from Malou, but she does give me an old chewed-up pen. She kisses me on the cheek. I guess it's a fair fee for her service.

I write on the back of Malou's last note, using the toilet seat as my desk. "Dad and Mom are going to get us out of here. My money is on Mom. Didn't get any new tattoos. Miss you, too. Strangely. Your brother."

I also write "Thinking of Zelda hurts," but then I scribble over it until you can't read the words anymore.

The male nurse pushes me into the Red Tie Man's office. Mom. Dad. Édouard. More nurses. Even Malou is already in there. They're all looking at me.

"What's going on?" I ask.

The Red Tie Man has a black eye and fresh scratches all over his face. He sits behind his desk, doing his best to produce his first smile in years.

"You and your stepsister are released into your father's custody." He sounds particularly smug for someone losing two of his favorite prisoners.

"But Zelda will stay here with us," he says, sending a massive electroshock down my spine.

"Zelda?" I turn to Malou for confirmation. "Zelda can't be here."

Malou nods her head sadly. "She came back for you, Frog."

The Red Tie Man is so intensely happy, his smile gets all twisted. "Do you know what schizophrenia is, David?"

I turn to Dad. I don't care what schizophrenia is. Zelda is not crazy. "Tell me he's lying. Tell me she's not locked up here."

Dad is incapable of lying. "She's here, David. I saw her. She's heavily drugged."

"We have her on antidepressants. She was very upset," the Red Tie Man says. He has a scratched face and black eye to illustrate his point. "But we can manage her violent behavior in here."

I'm staring at his red tie. Something nasty is rising up in me.

"Zelda belongs with us," he says.

I leap forward and land on the desk. The nurses try to drag me away. It's too late for that. I get a good hold on their boss's red tie. The more they pull me, the more the Red Tie Man screams like a girl. Even Dad begs me to let go of him.

I scream. Malou screams. Mom screams the most.

The nurses are pulling and punching me with renewed energy. They jerk me, squeeze me, and squash me. I can't breathe, but I'm okay with that as long as the Red Tie Man can't breathe either.

"Let me go," I whisper. They push and pull me harder, pinning me down on the desk with their knees. I spit out the last tiny bit of air in my lungs. I'm suffocating. If only I could take one last deep breath, I could finish him. Everything turns soft and yellow. I can't fight anymore. I let go of the tie.

And *poof*. Lights out.

When I come back to life, I'm in Dad's arms. He's carrying me like he did when I was a kid. He's practically running through the corridor, he's so eager to get me out of this place.

I can see Mom over his shoulders. "You nearly killed him, you idiots! I'll sue the ass off you!" she yells at the Red Tie Man, who follows us into the corridor, taking off his tie, coughing, and yelling harsh words.

He's gone from purple to simply red.

———

No one's talking in Édouard's car. No one mentions Mom's car and what we did to it. Dad sits between Malou and me in the backseat.

"Get her out of there," I say.

Dad never lies, and he tells it the way it is: "I can't get her out of there."

"Mom?"

She turns to me, hiding her eyes behind her large purple sunglasses again.

"Can you get her out of there?" I repeat.

She shakes her head. She can't get Zelda out, or she just doesn't want to.

"She's not crazy."

They pretend I didn't say anything.

"She's not schizophrenic. She's . . ."

"She's *what*?" Mom asks coldly.

"She's really from outer space," Malou answers for me.

"Say something!" Mom gives Dad a furious look. "You're the cuckoo expert."

"This is not about you and your stupid fights," I shout before Dad can explain that no one is ever cuckoo. "This is about Zelda. She needs my help."

"They're going to *help* her in that place," Mom says. "It's not your business, anyway."

She leans over to grab my arm and show the tattoo to Dad.

"I found a clinic that will laser this *thing* off."

I pull my arm away. "You're not touching it!"

She turns back to the highway. Her hands shake as she lights her next cigarette. She takes a few drags before she can speak again. "This crazy girl has turned my son into a terrorist."

Damn right. And I'll give them more terror. "Malou is coming back to live with us," I declare, like I'm in charge now.

Mom and Édouard exchange a look. They thought they could just drop her off anywhere in Paris and forget all about her.

"Maybe Malou doesn't want to live with us," Mom says hopefully.

"I don't want to be alone right now," Malou whispers.

"I guess she can live with us for a while," Mom concedes hesitantly, "if she promises not to touch any of my things or drive Édouard mental."

"I won't touch your things," Malou says. She can't promise anything about driving her father mental.

19

KEY TO VAHALAL LOCKED ON THE EARTHLING CREATURE CALLED DAVID GERSHWIN— VALIDITY: REMAINS UNLIMITED

"**W**ake up," I say, squatting in front of Malou in the middle of the night. She's sleeping on a mattress straight on the floor in the middle of my room. I give her a serious push.

"Wha-at?"

"You snore."

She moans. "You woke me up because I snore?"

"No, I woke you up because we're getting Zelda out."

Zap! That does it. Malou sits up as if the devil just poked her ass with his tail.

"Tadpole, you know I'm all for it. But that nuthouse is like a freaking prison."

I shrug. "I don't care. We're going back."

"It will take, like, an army to get Zelda out."

"Good. I know exactly where to find one."

"Oh *no no no*! You're not really thinking of those girls."

I'm *precisely* thinking of those girls. "Mom and Édouard are asleep. Hurry up." I throw her jeans on the mattress. "Are you in or out?"

"You don't want to involve the freaking Valks," she protests, but she starts pulling on her jeans. "Remember how they are: Kill this, destroy that!"

"Great!" I kick her sneakers toward her. "That's exactly the sort of attitude we need."

———

This time, we steal Édouard's cherished BMW SUV, since Mom's Mercedes is still impounded by the police.

"You'll see. He's totally going to blame this on me," Malou says, stopping the car in front of the abandoned school.

"They'll never know." I get out of the car and face the decaying building. Somehow it's even more sinister than I remembered. "When they wake up, we'll be sleeping in our room. The car will be in its parking place. Zelda will be in my closet."

Two Vahalalians spring out of their foxholes the second we pass the playground. Their faces are covered in markings. We're dealing with two angry Valks.

They squeak nervously, circling us, their batons in hand. "Look, they came back, the fools," they seem to say.

"We want to talk with the mother," I tell them, trying to avoid looking them in the eye.

Instead of answering, they start sniffing me like two hound dogs.

"Okay, that's disturbing," Malou whispers.

But we haven't seen anything yet. One of them grabs my hair, pulls my head back, and kisses me roughly.

"For Chrissake!" Malou pulls me away from the girl's embrace. "Easy now," she tells the second girl who's charging like she wants some, too.

But the second Vahalalian is not after a kiss. She lifts my sleeve and looks at my key tattoo and—*oh boy*! They start squeaking like dolphins eyeing a bucket of sardines.

———————

"They are right," the mother says as soon as we step into the gym, where she awaits us. She gets closer and sniffs me just like her watchdogs did. "You stink of it."

"Stink of what?"

"Check his tattoo! Check his tattoo!" the disciples seem to chant in their lingo, whirlpooling closer and closer around us on the basketball court. Even the failed Travelers get closer to me, some of them pinching me and my clothes like they want to chew off a piece of me.

"I need your help," I say. "Zelda is being held prisoner."

The mother isn't listening. She grabs my arm, lifts my sleeve, and checks my tattoo. "Clever girl," she sneers. "She transferred the key to you before it expired."

And to make absolutely sure I'm the real McCoy, she closes her eyes and . . . er . . . *samples* me.

Some of the Vahalalians howl and rattle the climbing ropes; they find all this extremely exciting.

"He's just a kid, you *vinyl freak*," Malou screams, trying to pull me away.

"Delicious," the mother whispers, licking her lips like she just tasted a great wine. "He has the key!" she yells.

And the girls go wild! They touch me. Pull my hair. Drag me this way and that, like they all want a piece of me.

Malou is holding me tight, trying to protect me from this pack of lunatics. "Frog, I'm going to be honest with you. I think they're going to eat you."

Ooouch. There's some truth to that. One of the failed Travelers just went on all fours and bit my left calf.

I turn to the mother and look her straight in the eyes. I don't care if it's a sin. "Help me get Zelda back," I beg. "I will give you the key. Even if it means . . . *transferring* it to you."

Ooouch. Another one bites me on the butt. Jeez, these girls are eager.

"I'll do anything you want if you free her."

The mother sneers, like, "isn't he cute?" and then she asks the million-dollar question: "Will you open the door to Vahalal for us?"

"I will," I say, moving away from a particularly voracious Traveler.

"So be it!" The mother raises her hand. Her disciples stop trying to eat me alive to listen to her. "Girls, pack up! We're going home."

"Woohoo!" they hoot collectively.

"Oh, one last thing." The mother turns to me with a wicked glint in her eye. "Did Zelda tell you how we open the door?"

"No."

"Let me tell you, Earthling," she says with a nasty smirk. "You're in for quite a ride."

———————

This feels just like a school field trip. Since all the exiles are coming to Zelda's rescue, the Valks stole two school buses to transport

159

everyone comfortably. We're zooming through the distant Parisian suburbs. The moon is up. I'm sitting beside Malou, thinking of Zelda.

The Vahalalians are singing beautiful songs in their dolphin dialect—a girls' soccer team celebrating a victory wouldn't look happier.

"We meet again, Earthling," a Vahalalian says, leaning over my seat and putting her hand on my shoulder. It's Lena. She looks much better, almost fully recovered from our trip down south.

"What are they singing?" Malou asks her.

"War songs. This one is about chopping your enemies' heads off and making trophies out of them."

The Red Tie Man and his goons are doomed.

––––––––

"I feel like murder!" the mother says, stepping off the bus holding two scary old axes. "Let the engine run. This won't take long."

"Just one more thing." I stop her before she charges with her troops.

"What?" she shouts.

"Actually, I'd really appreciate it if you wouldn't do the Ugo thing with those." I nod toward the axes.

"Why?"

"Consider it part of the deal. If you chop off anyone's head, I won't open the door."

"What about gutting?"

"Uh-uh."

"Cutting off limbs?"

"Afraid not."

"Killing at all?"

"Nope."

"Argh!" she groans and throws the axes on the ground, drawing her baton instead. "Girls! Find Zelda, destroy this place," she orders. "And, well, no killings!" she adds sadly.

I swear, the Valks moan in disappointment.

Twenty minutes later, every building is on fire and all the patients and nursing staff are running around the lawn like headless chickens.

"They know how to get things done," Malou says approvingly. We're leaning against the bus, watching the show. Even the failed Travelers are participating in their own way by chewing on bits of grass and dirt from the lawns.

Then I see her. My very own Vahalalian, dragged away from the mayhem by our old friends Lena and Pela.

Zelda! I'm flying, I'm overwhelmed, I'm running toward her, I'm—

"Don't do it, David!" Zelda screams the second she sees me. "Don't open the door for them! They'll—"

Pela claps a hand over her mouth, and they drag her onto the bus before she can say more.

The mother picks up her axes before getting into the bus. "Come now, babies." She kisses each blade. "We're going back to Vahalal."

20

KEY TO VAHALAL LOCKED ON THE EARTHLING CREATURE CALLED DAVID GERSHWIN— VALIDITY: REMAINS UNLIMITED

They drag Zelda to a seat in the back and duct-tape her mouth to make her stop screaming. The Valks guard her, and they won't let me talk to her.

"I want to see her," I say, but Lena won't budge.

"Why are you treating her like a prisoner?" I ask the mother as she passes by, counting her disciples like a teacher counting her pupils after a trip to the zoo.

"We're all in," the mother says, pretending she didn't hear me. "Driver! To the Temple of Zook."

My eyes meet with Zelda's.

"She's Space Flopped," the mother says. "Transferring the key is a very debilitating process."

Here is another piece of Vahalalianism: There are two things that cause Space Flop, intergalactic traveling and . . . well . . . doing it with an Earthling.

I look at Zelda. "Mmmm! Mmmm! Mmmm!" she moans, shaking her head.

"I'm not sure I want to do this anymore."

"What?" The mother turns to me, her good mood all gone.

"I think . . . Zelda doesn't want me to open the door."

"It's too late. We have a deal."

"I want to talk to Zelda. If you don't let me talk to her, I won't do it."

"How typical." The mother sighs. "It was such a lovely evening, and now you're ruining it." She grabs my neck in a flash and squeezes till I can't breathe. Pela grabs Malou and does the same thing to her before she can try to come to my rescue.

"Listen carefully," the mother says, pulling one of her beloved axes from its holster on her belt. She holds the edge dangerously close to my eyes. "You'll be begging to open the door when I start popping your eyes out." She scratches my cheek ever so slightly with the blade to give me a preview of what's to come. "Now sit tight and enjoy the ride."

––––––––––

They park the buses in the middle of the tiny rue des Oiseaux, in front of the Temple of Zook. They don't care about being discreet or getting a ticket; in a few minutes, they will be zooming through space and back to Vahalal! And they sure sing loudly about it, like a bunch of drunken sailors.

"I haven't been in here for five hundred years," the mother says, dragging me into the temple. She looks up at Zook and sighs sadly. "See that hole?" She points to the pit at the base of the painting. "It was made by all the Vahalalians trying to return without a valid key."

"How do I open it?" I ask, getting more and more anxious. "Do I show the key to your goddess? Do I rub it against the painting? Are you going to draw my blood?"

"That would be interesting." The mother smiles and taps my face. "But no, there will be no blood and no rubbing."

I turn around to Zelda. She's tied to a bench at the very back of the chapel, humming, fuming, and kicking.

"The secret to opening the door," the mother says gravely, "is speed."

"Speed?"

"You will Space Splash, collide into the wall at a very high speed, and before you know it, you'll find yourself in Vahalal. And, let me tell you from personal experience, it's better to hold a valid key if you don't want to end up with a bad concussion."

Wait a freaking minute! "I can't Space Splash!"

"Of course you can't. Tena, Lena, Pela," the mother calls, and the three Valks grab me by the arms and waist, ready to push me into the wall. "Since you Earthlings are so slow, they will help you reach critical speed." She gives them the *go go go!* sign with her baton. "See you in Vahalal."

"Wait!"

"What?!" She slams her baton against a bench, like I'm getting on her last nerve with all my hesitations.

"Don't they disintegrate all males except chosen ones the second they set foot on Vahalal?"

She rolls her eyes. "Yes, of course," she says. "But don't worry. Disintegration is painless."

Malou puts my general feeling about that in very simple words: "NO FREAKING WAY! You're not disintegrating Tadpole!"

"Mmmmmm-mmmmm!" Zelda moans.

I look at her sadly. She tried to warn me: Opening the door means turning into a heap of ashes.

"Ready?" Lena asks, holding me tight.

"WAIT!"

The mother growls angrily, raising her baton in the air, and looking like she's about to break something, possibly my head. "Wait? I've been waiting three thousand years on your stupid planet. Why would you want me to wait more?"

She's not close enough, not if I want to . . . "I need to tell you something. It's very important."

"Speak. Quick! And be done."

"It's also very personal." I wave my head, inviting her to get closer.

She sighs and takes one step closer, leaning so I can whisper my last words in her ear. I take a deep breath, and here goes! I yank my arm away from Lena and reach for the axes on the mother's belt. Bingo! I got one. I hold it aloft for everyone to see.

The mother looks at it and laughs. "You want to *fight*? With us?"

The other Vahalalians laugh, too, clapping their own axes, knives, and batons on the walls and benches. They find me irresistible with my ax and my grand delusions.

"I won't fight you." I turn to Zelda. "She will."

"Mm-mm!" agrees Zelda.

I close my eyes. We've been here before. Apples, marbles, or axes, it's all the same thing: Hit the target first, then throw and reverse time with your mind. It is basic psychophysics!

I throw the ax toward Zelda, aiming for a spot right beside her hand. The good news: I don't cut off any of her fingers. The bad news: I still throw like a Zokoplasm from planet Altar! The ax lands on the floor a good six feet away from her. Zelda looks up at me, shaking her head and moaning some inaudible harsh words. And the laughter gets louder.

"Entertaining," says the mother, still laughing, and walks down the aisle to retrieve her darling ax. "If I weren't in such a good mood, I'd cut off one of your hands just on principle."

"Cut *this*!" screams Malou, throwing herself on the ax and grabbing it first. She springs to her feet and—*slash!*—cuts the rope tying Zelda to the bench and—*ZAM!*—cuts the rope tying Zelda's hands. Zelda snatches the ax and walks down the aisle for a good, old-fashioned, one-on-one fight to the death.

Even the mother looks impressed. She draws the second ax, but instead of Space Splashing or charging, she turns to the girls holding me and gives them a small nod and a simple order. "Open the door."

They grab me tighter, and before I can say "Hold on there, guys," everything goes, like, *zooooooooooooooooom*!

You know, I was supposed to spend a quiet summer with my dad in Normandy, a hundred miles from Paris. No one told me I'd be shooting away from our galaxy and traveling to the far reaches of our universe.

Not that it's such a big deal, per se. It's fast. Instantaneous, for that matter. Like you start to scream "omigod!" on Earth and you finish spitting out the last syllable on Vahalal.

When Tena, Lena, and Pela let go of me, I look around and I know for a fact that we're not in *gai Paris* anymore.

I've got three words for you: *gold*, *silver*, and *gigantic*.

I can't focus my eyes on anything. The light's so intense it hurts.

There are a few things I know for sure:

1. We're surrounded by great columns of metal, rising all the way up into a deep, bright red sky.

2. Everywhere I look, I see girls clad in fancy silver swimsuits and gold jewelry.

3. They're squeaking up a storm.

When my eyes adjust to the strange light, I realize that the mother, queen of the exiles, is standing beside me, squeaking back at the girls in silver bikinis.

I don't speak dolphin, but I'd say disintegration is near.

———————

A huge shadow is cast upon us. I look up. Holy spaghetti! A flying thing shaped like a prehistoric bird is floating right above our heads. Girls in shiny silver armor glide down from the sky and land all around us. Their helmets are shaped like human skulls. The minute they set foot on the metallic floor, they start to squeak at an intolerably high pitch.

The exiles who have magically appeared all around me don't look too perky anymore. The armored girls draw metal disks and point them toward me, and since everyone starts to gasp and cry and back away from me, I'd say it doesn't necessarily look like good news.

"So long, Earthling," the mother says.

That's it! I want to go home.

"David!"

"Zelda? Where are you?"

I spin around, desperately searching for her. She stands right beside me. She drops the mother's ax on the floor and wraps her arms around me. "Close your eyes," she says. "I'm taking you home." The armored girls' disks are getting brighter. I think they're about to shoot. I close my eyes and hear a big sonic boom. Before I can start screaming, I feel this incredible pull dragging me back again: *mooooooooooZ.*

———————

We fall back on the stone floor of the Temple of Zook.

That's Temple of Zook, Paris, France, Earth, Galaxy zeta-7895.

I stare at the ceiling. The candles are making quite a show of light and shadow up there.

Malou's face appears above me. "Tadpole?" She pokes me. "Your girlfriend just . . . walked into the wall, and you . . . you fell out of it in her arms like a freaking ghost," she whispers. "This is so totally creepy."

I sit up and look around. All the Vahalalians have gone to the other side. There're only the three of us left on this side of the galaxy. I turn to Zelda. I still can't manage to focus my eyes on her face. I try to stand up, but my legs feel like two bags of jumbo marshmallows. I fall back on my ass.

"We're Space Flopped," Zelda explains, struggling to stand up. "It will pass." She dusts something off her arms . . . stardust, I suppose.

"That's where you want to drag Johnny Depp?" I ask, pointing to the painting of Zook. "He's not going to like it up there!"

She shakes her head. "He's never going to Vahalal. He's not my chosen one." She helps me stand up, holding me tight. "I went to his movie premiere. The one you talked about. I was hiding in the crowd waiting for him. I jumped out when he passed by, and I sampled him."

"You did what?!" Imagining my very own spacegirl smooching Johnny Depp feels like swallowing bleach.

"He tastes wrong," she says, ignoring my pained face. "Nearly as wrong as you, by the way, which proves once more that face recognition cannot be trusted."

Malou gasps. "You kissed Johnny Depp? Really? What did he have to say about that?"

"He's a strange Earthling. He laughed and walked away when I told him he was worthless."

"Do you know how many girls would have killed to be in your knee-high boots?" Malou shakes her head. "You're really a strange person, Zelda from the stars."

"So if he's not your guy . . . ?" I ask carefully.

And considering that you love me madly as proven by your attempt at saving my life and . . . giving me the key . . . and . . .

"My real chosen one is still out there, somewhere, and I will find him."

Oh no!

"Here we go again!" Malou complains.

"But . . ." I show her the octopus thingy on my arm. "I have the key, right? How would you give it to your chosen one?" I shake my head warily. Because if she mentions transferring it to him through . . . *the usual way*, I'm going to scream.

"We can't transfer it anymore," she admits, grabbing my arm and inspecting the tattoo. "It's locked on you forever, and only you can open that door for me. And you will, the day I find him."

"No way!" I pull my arm away. "I'm never going back there to be pulverized by a bunch of bikini girls so you can live happily ever after with a guy you don't even know."

"It's not your decision to make, Pudin. And if it makes you feel better about it, they will probably pulverize me too, for I have committed a deadly sin going back to Vahalal to save you. But I will plead for our lives and leave our fate to Zook."

Space Flopped or not, she's still very annoying. I grab her sweater with both hands. "YOU ARE IMPOSSIBLE, ZELDA!"

"Behave, Pudin, or I will hurt you."

"Guys!" Malou complains. "I know you have this cute S-and-M thing going on, but we better get away before the cops come to investigate those two buses parked outside."

To be continued. I let go of Zelda and try to take a few steps. But my knees are still wobbly, and I end up falling back into her arms. She doesn't push me away. Or yell at me. Or tell me I'm just a clumsy useless key doomed to be pulverized by bikini girls.

It's my cue to try something new and daring. Something an intergalactic traveler like me shouldn't be scared of.

I lift myself up, pull her body against mine, and kiss her—or sample her—right there in front of Zook.

And I don't care if she'll ever find her chosen one or if she'll throw me into that wall and let the Valks turn us into two heaps of ashes because of all the terrible sins we've committed. Because, personally, I see a thousand stars, and I know for sure that the universal balance has just been restored with a single smooch.

"GUUUUYS!" Malou shouts. "I hate to spoil *the moment*, but can we go hide someplace and *then* make out!?"

21

SOMEWHERE ON A BORING PLANET ON THE OUTSKIRTS OF GALAXY ZETA-7895 . . .

"Can you cover yourself? You're going to give Olivier another anxiety attack."

Malou shrugs and flips to her other side, sunbathing on the grass in the type of super-mini bikini that's already made Olivier's head explode on many occasions in the past. And then I'll have him crying on my shoulder for hours, begging me to pass her another of his love letters.

I've told him he's not her type. He's not middle-aged, he's far from anorexic, he hasn't done time in a mental or penal institution, and he doesn't look like he's into mass murder. All red flags for Malou.

"Your friend is obsessed." She sits up. "Do you know the sort of shit he writes in those letters? Like, I'm the caramel to his butter-scotch pudding!" She takes off her bikini top, exposing her *things* to the sun.

I hear someone screaming and falling in the neighboring garden. I have a pretty good idea what sort of UFO crash-landed the instant bazooms came into the landscape.

"Olivier? Are you all right?"

I walk to where I can see into his garden. Olivier is standing up, brushing dirt and grass from his knees and ass and clumsily picking up a ladder. I retrieve something that must have fallen on the ground during his plunge: his air gun.

"I was coming to get you. Frogs?" he asks, blushing.

"Can't." I give him back his air gun. "I have to go to therapy soon," I lie.

"Wait." He follows me back to my own garden. Freezes. Stops to breathe. Makes a face like Godzilla's mowing my lawn. Malou is still flashing her bazongas, singing and drumming the grass as she listens to her iPod.

"Did you give her my letter?" Olivier whispers, unable to take his eyes off her.

"I did." I carefully back away before he can start quizzing me— he might shoot a pellet through his heart when I tell him she's not into him.

"What did she say?"

"She was very intrigued by your food metaphors."

"Hey! Butterscotch boy!" Malou takes out one of her earbuds and throws her bottle of suntan lotion toward him. It lands in front of his feet. "Can you do my back?"

I leave them to it and run into the house, then check on them through the window to make sure Olivier hasn't died of spontaneous combustion. He's walking toward Malou in ultraslow motion, holding tight to the lotion. You can hear him swallowing saliva from sixty feet away.

I laugh and open the fridge, grabbing leftovers from lunch, a bottle of milk, and her absolute favorite: a pint of vanilla ice cream from the freezer. I pack all this in a plastic bag and head toward the back door. As I pass Dad's office, I can hear him snoring happily. I have a good three hours before he calls me and Malou in for afternoon snacks. (Dad's an afternoon-snacks fanatic and thinks a day isn't complete without a proper milk-and-cookie break.)

I stop under the apple tree in the back garden, then climb up and retrieve the baton Zelda made for me. I jump over the fence and run across Monsieur Dupuis's cornfield, knocking, kicking, clubbing, and shouldering the cornstalks like they're a thousand imaginary enemies.

––––––––––

"OUCH!" I scream, scaring some bats away. She clubbed me on the shoulder again.

"I said keep your guard up. And watch for my side blows." Zelda kicks some dust toward me with the tip of her boot, getting back into her combat stance. "Fight!"

"Wait. I need to finish rubbing my dead shoulder." The sun is beaming on the thick waves of nettles outside. A strong, warm wind flows in and out of the cave. "Can we do something else? I'd love to take another crack at bending time."

The wind blows her hair across her face. She brushes it away and smiles. "Sure. I'll bend time for you." And—*zaaam!*—she Space Splashes.

I hate when she does that!

She reappears right in front of me and goes for the head. I'm able to block that one. She keeps swinging. Left, right, front. *BAM!* Gets the same shoulder on the very same spot. My howling sends another family of bats looking for quieter parts of the cave.

"You're too predictable. Too slow." Zelda corrects my position with the tip of her baton. "Left leg forward. Bend your knees. Stomach in. Shoulders relaxed. Chin up, and . . . fight!"

"Stop!" I throw my baton away and sit down in the dust.

This old clay mine is our secret kingdom. The Cornouaillois never come here. It's supposed to be haunted since SS soldiers murdered and buried a group of resistance fighters here during World War II.

Zelda puts her baton away and sits beside me. "You have so much to learn to earn this." She takes my arm and checks the octopus tattoo. She says the key will transform me, in time. Make me more like her. Like, I might even be able to bend time and Space Splash one day.

"But you need to practice, practice, practice!"

I reach for the plastic bag and take out the pint of perfectly melted vanilla ice cream and two spoons.

"You think you're going to win me over with ice cream again?"

"Negative. I *know* I'm going to win you over with ice cream again," I say, opening the lid. "It's like a Vahalalian trap."

"Clever boy," she says, and we start spooning away, admiring the bats shooting out of the cave and then quickly flying back in to escape the sun. She leans against me and rests her head on my shoulder. I smile. I'm the key to her world. I might be slow, clumsy, and still unable to block her side blows, but I'm with her forever.

And, who knows? One day she might give up running on rooftops, smashing policemen's heads, and destroying cities searching for her chosen one. And I'll be right here waiting for her, eating vanilla ice cream and watching bats dance in the wind.

ACKNOWLEDGMENTS

Thanks to Mary Colgan at Chronicle Books for her commitment and exceptional insights; Kathryn Lye, Lynda Curnyn, Maria Ahlund, and Ruben Gerson for their kindness and warm support.

Also thanks to my wonderful agent, Marlene Stringer at the Stringer Literary Agency, for her unlimited enthusiasm and hard work.